THE OUTER LIMITS™

VOLUME ONE

Edited by

Debbie Notkin and Roger Stewart

BOXTREE

*To Tom Whitmore and Dave Nee,
who set me on the path that turned
a passion into a profession*
—*Debbie*

To Laurie and Rachel
—*Roger*

First published in the USA by Prima Publishing

This edition published in 1997 by Boxtree
an imprint of Macmillan Publishers Ltd
25 Eccleston Place, London SW1W 9NF
and Basingstoke

Associated companies throughout the world.

ISBN: 0 7522 0274 X

Copyright © 1997 Outer Limits Productions Inc., in trust.
All Rights Reserved. The Outer Limits is a trademark of
Metro-Goldwyn-Mayer Inc., and is licensed by MGM/UA
Licensing and Merchandising.

Copyright notice:
"Soldier" by Harlan Ellison. Copyright © 1957 by Harlan
Ellison. Renewed, copyright © 1985 by Harlan Ellison.
Reprinted by arrangement with, and permission of, the
Author and the Author's agent, Richard Curtis Associates,
Inc., New York. All rights reserved.

All rights reserved. No reproduction, copy or transmission
of this publication may be made without written permission.
No paragraph of this publication may be reproduced, copied or
transmitted save with the written permission or in accordance with
the provisions of the Copyright Act 1956 (as amended). Any
person who does any unauthorized act in relation to
this publication may be liable to criminal prosecution
and civil claims for damages.

9 8 7 6 5 4 3 2 1

A CIP record for this book is available from the British Library

Printed and bound in Great Britain by
Mackays of Chatham plc, Chatham, Kent

Contents

Introduction iv

SOLDIER 1
  Harlan Ellison

IT CRAWLED OUT OF THE WOODWORK 37
  Diane Duane

IF THESE WALLS COULD TALK 115
  Howard Hendrix

THE SIXTH FINGER 193
  John M. Ford

Introduction

THE *OUTER LIMITS* was on television in the mid-1960s for less than two seasons.

This simple statement of fact comes as a shock to most people. If you are a science fiction fan and a Baby Boomer, the chances are very good indeed that you remember *The Outer Limits* vividly. Indeed, the series resonates in memory with an impact that is far greater than the handful of episodes (only forty-eight) that aired before the show ended.

While the classic series lives on, evergreen on home video, the people at MGM/UA have—to their immense credit—seen fit to breathe new life into *The Outer Limits* with all-new episodes that evoke the chills and thrills of the original series. Winner of the coveted CableACE Award for Best Dramatic Series, the new

Outer Limits brings to a younger generation all the mind-expanding extrapolations, cautionary lessons, and fright-inducing "bears" (as Joseph DeStefano was wont to call his trademark bogeymen) that we associate with the best of *The Outer Limits*.

This series of print anthologies, of which you hold the first volume in your hands, adapts into print for the first time anywhere episodes from both the classic and the new *Outer Limits* series. In addition to new adaptations by top-flight authors such as Diane Duane, John M. Ford, and others, this series also includes reprints of classic original short stories by notable authors such as Harlan Ellison and Fredric Brown that were adapted into unforgettable screenplays for the original *Outer Limits* series.

Now sit back and relax while we control what you see and hear . . . .

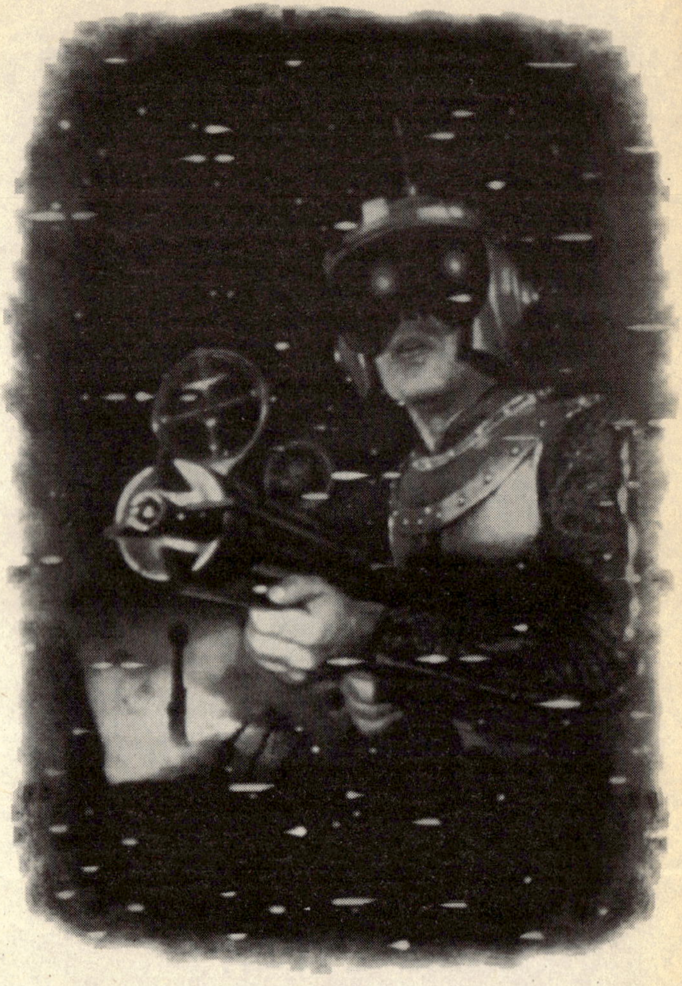

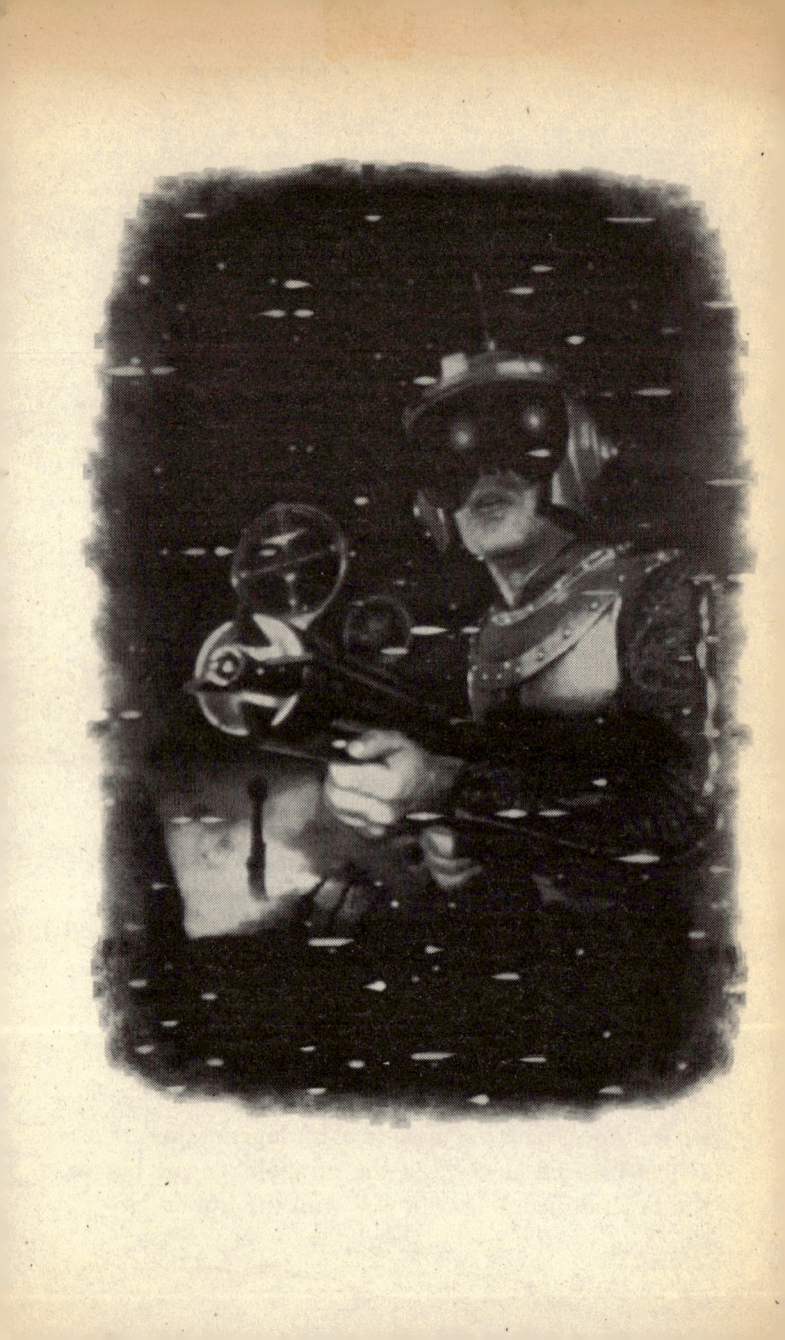

A soldier on a battlefield can be a denizen of the past, the present, or the future. His fears can be arrows or musket shot, bullets from automatic weapons, or the undiscovered projectiles to come. His orders can come shouted from the duke on horseback, spoken into his cellular communication devices, or sent telepathically from an offsite commander.

But the things he faces are the things soldiers have faced since time immemorial: Will I be killed? Will I have to kill? Will I be maimed? Will I be able to face the terrors I'm about to encounter? What is to become of me?

"Soldier" is a classic of the military science fiction sub-genre, on which the famous 1964 Outer Limits *episode (also written by Harlan Ellison) was based. In this case, unlike the other stories in this book, the story came before the screenplay.*

Soldier

Harlan Ellison

QARLO HUNKERED down further into the firmhole, gathering his cloak about him. Even the triple-lining of the cape could not prevent the seeping cold of the battlefield from reaching him; and even through one of those linings—lead impregnated—he could feel the faint tickle of dropout, all about him, eroding his body, pulverizing his bones, eating the marrow. He began to shiver again. The Push was going on to the South; and he had to wait; had to listen for the telepathic command of his superior officer.

He fingered an edge of the firmhole, noting he had not steadied it up too well with the firmer. He drew the small molecule-hardening instrument from his pouch, and examined it. The calibrator had slipped a notch; that explained why the dirt of the firmhole had not become as hard as he had desired.

Off to the left the hiss of an eighty-thread beam split the night air, and he shoved the firmer back quickly. The spiderweb tracery of the beam lanced across the sky, poked tentatively at an armor center, throwing blood-red shadows across Qarlo's crag-like features.

The armor center backtracked the thread beam, retaliated with a blinding flash of its own batteries. One burst. Two. Three. The eighty-thread reared once more, feebly, then subsided. A moment later the concussion of its power chambers exploding shook the Earth around Qarlo, causing bits of unfirmed dirt and small pebbles to tumble in on him. Another moment, and the shrapnel came through.

Qarlo lay flat to the ground, soundlessly hoping for a bit more life amidst all this death. He knew his chances of coming back were infinitesimal. What was it? Three out of every thousand came back? He had no illusions. He was a common footman, and he knew he would die out here, in the midst of the Great War VII.

As though the detonation of the eighty-thread had been a signal, the weapons of Qarlo's company opened up, full-on. The webbings crisscrossed the blackness overhead with delicate patterns—appearing, disappearing, changing with every second, ranging through the spectrum, washing the bands of color outside the spectrum Qarlo could catalog. Qarlo slid into a tiny ball in the slush-filled bottom of the firmhole, waiting.

He was a good soldier. He knew his place. When those metal and energy beasts out there were snarling at each other, there was nothing a lone foot soldier could do—but die. He waited, knowing his time would come much too soon. No matter how violent, how involved, how pushbutton-ridden Wars became, it always simmered down to the man on foot. It had to, for men fought men still.

His mind dwelled limply in a state between reflection and alertness. A state all men of war came to know when there was nothing but the thunder of the big guns abroad in the night.

The stars had gone into hiding.

Abruptly, the thread beams cut out, the traceries winked off, silence once again descended. Qarlo snapped to instant attentiveness. This was the moment. His mind was now keyed to one sound, one only. Inside his head the command would form, and he would act; not entirely of his own volition. The strategists and psychmen had worked together on this thing: the tone of command was keyed into each soldier's brain. Printed in, probed in, sunken in. It was there, and when the Regimenter sent his telepathic orders, Qarlo would leap like a puppet, and advance on direction.

Thus, when it came, it was as though he had anticipated it; as though he knew a second before the mental rasping and the *Advance!* erupted within his skull, that the moment had arrived.

A second sooner than he should have been, he was up, out of the firmhole, hugging his Brandelmeier to his chest, the weight of the plastic bandoliers and his pouch reassuring across his stomach, back, and hips. Even before the mental word actually came.

Because of this extra moment's jump on the command, it happened, and it happened just that way. No other chance coincidences could have done it, but done just that way.

When the first blasts of the enemy's zeroed-in batteries met the combined rays of Qarlo's own guns, also pinpointed, they met at a point that should by all rights have been empty. But Qarlo had jumped too soon, and when they met, the soldier was the focal point.

Three hundred distinct beams latticed down, joined in a coruscating rainbow, threw negatively charged particles five hundred feet in the air, shorted out . . . and warped the soldier off the battlefield.

~~~~~~~~~~

Nathan Schwachter had his heart attack right there on the subway platform.

The soldier materialized in front of him, from nowhere, filthy and ferocious-looking, a strange weapon cradled to his body . . . just as the old man was about to put a penny in the candy machine.

Qarlo's long cape was still, the dematerialization and subsequent reappearance having left him untouched. He stared in confusion at the sallow face before him, and started violently at the face's piercing shriek.

Qarlo watched with growing bewilderment and

terror as the sallow face contorted and sank to the littered floor of the platform. The old man clutched his chest, twitched and gasped several times. His legs jerked spasmodically, and his mouth opened wildly again and again. He died with mouth open, eyes staring at the ceiling.

Qarlo looked at the body disinterestedly for a moment; death . . . what did one death matter . . . every day during the War, ten thousand died . . . more horribly than this . . . this was as nothing to him.

The sudden universe-filling scream of an incoming express train broke his attention. The black tunnel that his War-filled world had become, was filled with the rusty wail of an unseen monster, bearing down on him out of the darkness.

The fighting man in him made his body arch, sent it into a crouch. He poised on the balls of his feet, his rifle levering horizontal instantly, pointed at the sound.

From the crowds packed on the platform, a voice rose over the thunder of the incoming train:

"*Him!* It was *him!* He shot that old man . . . he's crazy!" Heads turned; eyes stared; a little man with a dirty vest, his bald head reflecting the glow of the overhead lights, was pointing a shaking finger at Qarlo.

It was as if two currents had been set up simultaneously. The crowd both drew away and advanced on him. Then the train barreled around the curve, drove past, blasting sound into the very fibers of the soldier's body. Qarlo's mouth opened wide in a soundless scream, and more from reflex than intent, the Brandelmeier erupted in his hands.

A triple-thread of cold blue beams sizzled from the small bell mouth of the weapon, streaked across the tunnel, and blasted full into the front of the train.

The front of the train melted down quickly, and the vehicle ground to a stop. The metal had been melted like a coarse grade of plastic on a burner. Where it had fused into a soggy lump, the metal was bright and smeary—more like the gleam of oxidized silver that anything else.

Qarlo regretted having fired the moment he felt the Brandelmeier buck. He was not where he should be—where he *was,* that was still another, more pressing problem—and he knew he was in danger. Every movement had to be watched as carefully as possible . . . and perhaps he had gotten off to a bad start already. But that noise . . .

He had suffered the screams of the battlefield, but the reverberations of the train, thundering back and forth in that enclosed space, a nightmare of indescribable horror.

As he stared dumbly at his handiwork, from behind him, the crowd made a concerted rush.

Three burly, charcoal-suited executives—each carrying an attaché case which he dropped as he made the lunge, looking like unhealthy carbon-copies of each other—grabbed Qarlo above the elbows, around the waist, about the neck.

The soldier roared something unintelligible and flung them from him. One slid across the platform on the seat of his pants, bringing up short, his stomach and face smashing into a tiled wall. The second spun away, arms flailing, into the crowd. The third tried to hang onto Qarlo's neck. The soldier lifted him bodily, arched him over his head—breaking the man's insecure grip—and pitched him against a stanchion. The executive hit the girder, slid down, and lay quite still, his back oddly twisted.

The crowd emitted scream after scream, drew away once more. Terror rippled back through its ranks. Several women, near the front, suddenly became aware of the blood pouring from the face of one of the executives, and keeled onto the dirty platform unnoticed. The screams continued, seeming echoes of the now-dead express train's squealing.

But as an entity, the crowd backed the soldier down the platform. For a moment Qarlo forgot he still held the Brandelmeier. He lifted the gun to a threatening position, and the entity that was the crowd pulsed back.

Nightmare! It was all some sort of vague, formless nightmare to Qarlo. This was not the War, where anyone he saw, he blasted. This was something else, some other situation, in which he was lost, disoriented. What was happening?

Qarlo moved toward the wall, his back prickly with fear sweat. He had expected to die in the War, but something as simple and direct and expected as that had not happened. He was *here*, not *there*—wherever *here* was, and wherever *there* had gone—and these people were unarmed, obviously civilians. Which would not have kept him from murdering them . . . but what was happening? Where was the battlefield?

His progress toward the wall was halted momentarily as he backed cautiously around a stanchion. He knew there were people behind him, as well as the white-faced knots before him, and he was beginning to suspect there was no way out. Such confusion boiled up in his thoughts, so close to hysteria was he—plain soldier of the fields—that his mind forcibly rejected the impossibility of being somehow transported from the War into this new—and in many ways more terrifying—situation. He concentrated on one thing only, as a good soldier should: *Out!*

He slid along the wall, the crowd flowing before him, opening at his approach, closing in behind. He whirled once, driving them back farther with the black hole of the Brandelmeier's bell mouth. Again he hesitated (not knowing why) to fire upon them.

He sensed they were enemies. But still they were unarmed. And yet, that had never stopped him before. The village in TetraOmsk Territory, beyond the Volga somewhere. They had been unarmed there, too, but the square had been filled with civilians he had not hesitated to burn. Why was he hesitating now?

The Brandelmeier continued in its silence.

Qarlo detected a commotion behind the crowd, above the crowd's inherent commotion. And a movement. Something was happening there. He backed tightly against the wall as a blue-suited, brass-buttoned man broke through the crowd.

The man took one look, caught the unwinking black eye of the Brandelmeier, and threw his arms back, indicating to the crowd to clear away. He began screaming at the top of his lungs, veins standing out in his temples, "Geddoudahere! The guy's a cuckaboo! Somebody'll get kilt! Beat it, run!"

The crowd needed no further impetus. It broke in the center and streamed toward the stairs.

Qarlo swung around, looking for another way out, but both accessible stairways were clogged by fighting commuters, shoving each other mercilessly to get out. He was effectively trapped.

The cop fumbled at his holster. Qarlo caught a glimpse of the movement from the corner of his eye. Instinctively he knew the movement for what it was; a weapon was about to be brought into use. He swung about, leveling the Brandelmeier. The cop jumped behind a stanchion just as the soldier pressed the firing stud.

A triple-thread of bright blue energy leaped from the weapon's bell mouth. The beam went over the heads of the crowd, neatly melting away a five foot segment of wall supporting one of the stairways. The stairs creaked, and the sound of tortured metal adjusting to poor support and an overcrowding of people, rang through the tunnel. The cop looked fearfully above himself, saw the beams curving, then settle under the weight, and turned a wide-eyed stare back at the soldier.

The cop fired twice, from behind the stanchion, the booming of the explosions catapulting back and forth in the enclosed space.

The second bullet took the soldier above the wrist in his left arm. The Brandelmeier slipped uselessly from his good hand, as blood stained the garment he wore. He stared at his shattered lower arm in amazement. Doubled amazement.

What manner of weapon was this, the blue-coated man had used? No beam, that. Nothing like anything he had ever seen before. No beam to fry him in his tracks. It was some sort of power that hurled a projectile . . . that had ripped his body. He stared stupidly as blood continued to flow out of his arm.

The cop, less anxious now to attack this man with the weird costume and unbelievable rifle, edged cautiously from behind his cover, skirting the edge of the platform, trying to get near enough to Qarlo to put another bullet into him, should he offer further resistance. But the soldier continued to stand, spraddle-legged, staring at his wound, confused at where he was, what had happened to him, the screams of the trains as they bulleted past, and the barbarian tactics of his blue-coated adversary.

The cop moved slowly, steadily, expecting the soldier to break and run at any moment. The wounded man stood rooted, however. The cop bunched his muscles and leaped the few feet intervening.

Savagely, he brought the barrel of his pistol down on the side of Qarlo's neck, near the ear. The soldier turned slowly, anchored in his tracks, and stared unbelievingly at the policeman for an instant.

Then his eyes glazed, and he collapsed to the platform.

As a gray swelling mist bobbed up around his

mind, one final thought impinged incongruously: *he struck me . . . physical contact? I don't believe it!*

What have I gotten into?

~~~~~~~~~~~~~~

Light filtered through vaguely. Shadows slithered and wavered, sullenly formed into solids.

"Hey, Mac. Got a light?"

Shadows blocked Qarlo's vision, but he knew he was lying on his back, staring up. He turned his head, and a wall oozed into focus, almost at his nose tip. He turned his head the other way. Another wall, about three feet away, blending in his sight into a shapeless gray blotch. He abruptly realized the back of his head hurt. He moved slowly, swiveling his head, but the soreness remained. Then he realized he was lying on some hard metal surface, and he tried to sit up. The pains throbbed higher, making him feel nauseated, and for an instant his vision receded again.

Then it steadied, and he sat up slowly. He swung his legs over the sharp edge of what appeared to be a shallow, sloping metal trough. It was a mattressless bunk, curved in its bottom, from hundreds of men who had lain there before him.

He was in a cell.

"Hey! I said you got a match there?"

Qarlo turned from the empty rear wall of the cell and looked through the bars. A bulb-nosed face was thrust up close to the metal barrier. The man was short, in filthy rags whose odor reached Qarlo with tremendous offensiveness. The man's eyes were bloodshot, and his nose was crisscrossed with blue and red veins. Acute alcoholism, reeking from every pore; *acne rosacea* that had turned his nose into a hideous cracked and pocked blob.

Qarlo knew he was in detention, and from the very look, the very smell of this other, he knew he was not in a military prison. The man was staring in at him, oddly.

"Match, Charlie? You got a match?" He puffed his fat, wet lips at Qarlo, forcing the bit of cigarette stub forward with his mouth. Qarlo stared back; he could not understand the man's words. They were so slowly spoken, so sharp yet unintelligible. But he knew what to answer.

"Marnames Qarlo Clobregnny, pyrt, sizfifwunohtootoonyn," the soldier muttered by rote, surly tones running together.

"Whaddaya mad at *me* for, buddy? I didn't putcha in here," argued the match-seeker. "All I wanted was a light for this here butt." He held up two inches of smoked stub. "How come they gotcha inna cell, and not runnin' around loose inna bull pen like us?" He cocked a thumb over his shoulder, and for the first time Qarlo realized others were in this jail.

"Ah, to hell wit ya," the drunk muttered. He cursed again, softly under his breath, turning away. He walked across the bull pen and sat down with the four other men—all vaguely similar in facial content—who lounged around a rough-hewn table-bench combination.

The table and benches, all one piece, like a picnic table, were bolted to the floor.

"A screwloose," the drunk said to the others, nodding his balding head at the soldier in his long cape and metallic skintight suit. He picked up the crumpled remnants of an ancient magazine and leafed through it as though he knew every line of type, every girlie illustration, by heart.

Qarlo looked over the cell. It was about ten feet high by eight across, a sink with one thumb-push spigot running cold water, a commode without seat or paper, and metal trough, roughly the dimensions of an average-sized man, fastened to one wall. One enclosed bulb burned feebly in the ceiling. Three walls of solid steel. Ceiling and floor of the same, riveted together at the seams. The fourth wall was the barred door.

The firmer might be able to wilt that steel, he realized, and instinctively reached for his pouch. It was the first moment he had had a chance to think of it, and even as he reached, knew the satisfying weight of it was gone. His bandoliers also. His Brandelmeier, of course. His boots, too, and there seemed to have been some attempt to get his cape off, but it was all part of the skintight suit of metallic-mesh cloth.

The loss of the pouch was too much. Everything that had happened, had happened so quickly, so blurrily, meshed, and the soldier was abruptly overcome by confusion and a deep feeling of hopelessness. He sat down on the bunk, the ledge of the metal biting into his thighs. His head still ached from a combination of the blow dealt him by the cop, and the metal bunk where he had lain. He ran a shaking hand over his head, feeling the fractional inch of his brown hair, cut battle-style. Then he noticed that his left hand had been bandaged quite expertly. There was hardly any throbbing from his wound.

That brought back to sharp awareness all that had transpired, and the War leaped into his thoughts. The telepathic command, the rising from the firmhole, the rifle at the ready . . .

. . . then a sizzling shussssss, and the universe had exploded around him in a billion tiny flickering novas of color and color and color. Then suddenly, just as suddenly as he had been standing on the battlefield of Great War VII, advancing on the enemy forces of Ruskie-Chink, he was *not* there.

He was here.

He was in some dark, hard tunnel, with a great beast roaring out of the blackness onto him, and a man in a blue coat had shot him, and clubbed him. Actually *touched* him! Without radiation gloves! How had the man known Qarlo was not booby-trapped with radiates? He could have died in an instant.

Where was he? What war was this he was engaged in? Were these Ruskie-Chink or his own Tri-Continenters? He did not know, and there was no sign of an explanation.

Then he thought of something more important. If he had been captured, then they must want to question him. There was a way to combat *that*, too. He felt around in the hollow tooth toward the back of his mouth. His tongue touched each tooth till it hit the right lower bicuspid. It was empty. The poison glob was gone, he realized in dismay. *It must have dropped out when the blue-coat clubbed me*, he thought.

He realized he was at *their* mercy; who *they* might be was another thing to worry about. And with the glob gone, he had no way to stop their extracting information. It was bad. Very bad, according to the warning conditioning he had received. They could use Probers, or dyoxl-scopalite, or hypno-scourge, or any one of a hundred different methods, any one of which would reveal to them the strength of numbers in his company, the battery placements, the gun ranges, the identity and thought wave band of every officer . . . in fact, a good deal. More than he had thought he knew.

He had become a very important prisoner of War. He *had* to hold out, he realized!

Why?

The thought popped up, and was gone. All it left in its wake was the intense feeling: I despise War, all war and *the* War! Then, even that was gone, and he was alone with the situation once more, to try and decide what had happened to him . . . what secret weapon had been used to capture him . . . and if these unintelligible barbarians with the projectile weapons *could*, indeed, extract his knowledge from him.

I swear they won't get anything out of me but my name, rank, and serial number, he thought desperately.

He mumbled those particulars aloud, as reassurance: "Marnames Qarlo Clobregnny, pryt, sizfifwunoh-tootoonyn."

The drunks looked up from their table and their

shakes, at the sound of his voice. The man with the rosedrop nose rubbed a dirty hand across his fleshy chin folds, repeated his philosophy of the strange man in the locked cell.

"Screwloose!"

———∿∿∿∿∿∿∿∿———

He might have remained in jail indefinitely, considered a madman or a mad rifleman. But the desk sergeant who had booked him, after the soldier had received medical attention, grew curious about the strangely shaped weapon.

As he put the things into security, he tested the Brandelmeier—hardly realizing what knob or stud controlled its power, never realizing what it could do—and melted away one wall of the safe room. Three inch plate steel, and it melted bluely, fused solidly.

He called the Captain, and the Captain called the F.B.I., and the F.B.I. called Internal Security, and Internal Security said, "Preposterous!" and checked back. When the Brandelmeier had been thoroughly tested—as much as *could* be tested, since the rifle had no seams, no apparent power source, and fantastic range—they were willing to believe. They had the soldier removed from his cell, transported along with the pouch, and a philologist named Soames, to the I.S. general headquarters in Washington, D.C. The Brandelmeier came by jet courier, and the soldier was flown in by helicopter, under sedation. The philologist named Soames, whose hair was long and rusty, whose face was that of starving artist, whose temperament was that of a saint, came in by a specially chartered plane from Columbia University. The pouch was sent by sealed Brinks truck to the airport, where it was delivered under heaviest guard to a mail plane. They all arrived in Washington within ten minutes of one another, and without seeing anything of the surrounding countryside, were whisked away to the subsurface levels of the I.S. Buildings.

When Qarlo came back to consciousness, he found himself again in a cell, this time quite unlike the first. No bars, but just as solid to hold him in, with padded walls. Qarlo paced around the cell a few times, seeking breaks in the walls, and found what was obviously a door, in one corner. But he could not work his fingers between the pads, to try and open it.

He sat down on the padded floor, and rubbed the bristled top of his head in wonder. Was he never to find out what had happened to himself? And *when* was he going to shake this strange feeling that he was being watched?

~~~~~~~~~~~~~

Overhead, through a pane of one-way glass that looked like a ventilator grille, the soldier was being watched.

Lyle Sims and his secretary knelt before the window in the floor, along with the philologist named Soames. Where Soames was shaggy, ill-kept, hungry-looking and placid . . . Lyle Sims was lean, collegiate-seeming, brusque and brisk. He had been special advisor to an unnamed branch office of Internal Security, for five years, dealing with every strange or offbeat problem to outré for regulation inquiry. Those years had hardened him in an odd way; he was quick to recognize authenticity, even quicker to recognize fakery.

As he watched, his trained instincts took over completely, and he knew in a moment of spying, that the man in the cell below was out of the ordinary. Not so in any fashion that could be labeled—"drunkard," "foreigner," "psychotic"—but so markedly different, so *other*, he was taken aback.

"Six feet three inches," he recited to the girl kneeling beside him. She made the notation on her pad, and he went on calling out characteristics of the soldier below. "Brown hair, clipped so short you can see the scalp. Brown . . . no, black eyes. Scars. Above the left eye, running down to center of left cheek; bridge of nose; three parallel scars on the right side of chin; tiny one over right eyebrow; last one I can see, runs from back of left ear, into hairline.

"He seems to be wearing an all-over, skintight suit something like, oh, I suppose it's like a pair of what do you call those pajamas kids wear . . . the kind with the back door, the kind that enclose the feet?"

The girl inserted softly, "You mean snuggies?"

The man nodded, slightly embarrassed for no good reason, continued, "Mmm. Yes, that's right. Like those. The suit encloses his feet, seems to be joined to the cape, and comes up to his neck. Seems to be some sort of metallic cloth.

"Something else . . . may mean nothing at all, or on the other hand . . ." He pursed his lips for a moment, then described his observation carefully. "His head seems to be oddly shaped. The forehead is larger than most, seems to be pressing forward in front, as though he had been smacked hard and it was swelling. That seems to be everything."

Sims settled back on his haunches, fished in his side pocket, and came up with a small pipe, which he cold-puffed in thought for a second. He rose slowly, still staring down through the floor window. He murmured something to himself, and when Soames asked what he had said, the special advisor repeated, "I think we've got something almost too hot to handle."

Soames clucked knowingly, and gestured toward the window. "Have you been able to make out anything he's said yet?"

Sims shook his head. "No. That's why you're here. It seems he's saying the same thing, over and over, but it's completely unintelligible. Doesn't seem to be any recognizable language, or any dialect we've been able to pin down."

"I'd like to take a try at him," Soames said, smiling gently. It was the man's nature that challenge brought satisfaction; solution brought unrest, eagerness for a new, more rugged problem.

Sims nodded agreement, but there was a tense, strained film over his eyes, in the set of his mouth.

"Take it easy with him, Soames. I have a strong hunch this is something completely new, something we haven't even begun to understand."

Soames smiled again, this time indulgently. "Come, come, Mr. Sims. After all . . . he is only an alien of some sort . . . all we have to do is find out what country he's from."

"Have you heard him talk yet?"

Soames shook his head.

"Then don't be too quick to think he's just a foreigner. The word *alien* may be more correct than you think—only not in the *way* you think."

A confused look spread across Soames's face. He gave a slight shrug, as though he could not fathom what Lyle Sims meant . . . and was not particularly interested. He patted Sims reassuringly, which brought an expression of annoyance to the advisor's face, and he clamped down on the pipestem harder.

They walked downstairs together; the secretary left them, to type her notes, and Sims let the philologist into the padded room, cautioning him to deal gently with the man. "Don't forget," Sims warned, "we're not sure *where* he comes from, and sudden movements may make him jumpy. There's a guard overhead, and there'll be a man with me behind this door, but you never know."

Soames looked startled. "You sound as though he's an aborigine or something. With a suit like that, he *must* be very intelligent. You suspect something, don't you?"

Sims made a neutral motion with his hands. "What I suspect is too nebulous to worry about now.

Just take it easy . . . and above all, figure out what he's saying, where he's from."

Sims had decided, long before, that it would be wisest to keep the power of the Brandelmeier to himself. But he was fairly certain it was not the work of a foreign power. The trial run on the test range had left him gasping, confused.

He opened the door, and Soames passed through, uneasily.

Sims caught a glimpse of the expression on the stranger's face as the philologist entered. It was even more uneasy than Soames's had been.

It looked to be a long wait.

~~~~~~~~~~

Soames was white as library paste. His face was drawn, and the complacent attitude he had shown since his arrival in Washington was shattered. He sat across from Sims, and asked him in a quavering voice for a cigarette. Sims fished around in his desk, came up with a crumpled pack and idly slid them across to Soames. The philologist took one, put it in his mouth, then, as though it had been totally forgotten in the space of a second, he removed it, held it while he spoke.

His tones were amazed. "Do you know what you've got up there in that cell?"

Sims said nothing, knowing what was to come would not startle him too much; he had expected something fantastic.

"That man . . . do you know where he . . . that soldier—and by God, Sims, that's what he *is*—comes from, from—now you're going to think I'm insane to believe it, but somehow I'm convinced—he comes from the future!"

Sims tightened his lips. Despite himself, he *was* shocked. He knew it was true. It *had* to be true, it was the only explanation that fit all the facts.

"What can you tell me?" he asked the philologist.

"Well, at first I tried solving the communications problem by asking him simple questions . . . pointing to myself and saying 'Soames,' pointing to him and looking quizzical, but all he'd keep saying was a string of gibberish. I tried for hours to equate his tones and phrases with all the dialects and subdialects of every language I'd ever known, but it was no use. He slurred too much. And then I finally figured it out. He had to write it out—which I couldn't understand, of course, but it gave me a clue—and then I kept having him repeat it. Do you know what he's speaking?"

Sims shook his head.

The linguist spoke softly, "He's speaking English. It's that simple. Just English.

"But an English that has been corrupted and run together, and so slurred, it's incomprehensible. It must be the future trend of the language. Sort of an extrapolation of gutter English, just contracted to a fantastic extreme. At any rate, I got it out of him."

Sims leaned forward, held his dead pipe tightly. "What?"

Soames read it off a sheet of paper:

Soldier 23

"My name is Qarlo Clobregnny. Private. Six-five-one-oh-two-two-nine."

Sims murmured in astonishment. "My God . . . name, rank and—"

Soames finished for him, "—and serial number. Yes, that's all he'd give me for over three hours. Then I asked him a few innocuous questions, like where did he come from, and what was his impression of where he was now."

The philologist waved a hand vaguely. "By that time, I had an idea what I was dealing with, though not where he had come from. But when he began telling me about the War, the War he was fighting when he showed up here, I knew immediately he was either from some other world—which is fantastic—or, or . . . well, I just don't know!"

Sims nodded his head in understanding. "From *when* do you think he comes?"

Soames shrugged. "Can't tell. He says the year he is in—doesn't seem to realize he's in the past—is K79. He doesn't know when the other style of dating went out. As far as he knows, it's been 'K' for a long time, though he's heard stories about things that happened during a time they dated 'GV'. Meaningless, but I'd wager it's more thousands of years than we can imagine."

Sims ran a hand nervously through his hair. The problem was, indeed, larger than he'd thought.

"Look, Professor Soames, I want you to stay with him, and teach him current English. See if you can work some more information out of him, and let him know we mean him no hard times.

"Though Lord knows," the special advisor added with a tremor, "*he* can give us a harder time than we can give him. What knowledge he must have!"

Soames nodded in agreement. "Is it all right if I catch a few hours' sleep? I was with him almost ten hours straight, and I'm sure *he* needs it as badly as I do."

Sims nodded also, in agreement, and the philologist went off to a sleeping room. But when Sims looked down through the window, twenty minutes later, the soldier was still awake, still looking about nervously. It seemed he did *not* need sleep.

Sims was terribly worried, and the coded telegram he had received from the President, in answer to his own, was not at all reassuring. The problem was in his hands, and it was an increasingly worrisome problem.

Perhaps a deadly problem.

He went to another sleeping room, to follow Soames's example. It looked like sleep was going to be scarce.

~~~~~~~~~~

Problem:

A man from the future. An ordinary man, without any special talents, without any great store of intelligence. The equivalent of "the man in the street." A man who owns a fantastic little machine that turns sand into solid matter, harder than steel—but who hasn't the vaguest notion of how it works, or how to analyze it. A man whose knowledge of past history is as vague and formless as any modern man's. A soldier. With no other talent than fighting. What is to be done with such a man?

Solution:

Unknown.

Lyle Sims pushed the coffee cup away. If he ever had to look at another cup of the disgusting stuff, he was sure he would vomit. Three sleepless days and nights, running on nothing but dexedrine and hot black coffee, had put his nerves more on edge than usual. He snapped at the clerks and secretaries, he paced endlessly, and he had ruined the stems of five pipes. He felt muggy and his stomach was queasy. Yet there was no solution.

It was impossible to say, "All right, we've got a man from the future. So what? Turn him loose and let him make a life for himself in our time, since he can't return to his own."

It was impossible to do that for several reasons: (1) What if he *couldn't* adjust? He was then a potential menace, of *incalculable* potential. (2) What if an enemy power—and God knows there were enough powers around anxious to get a secret weapon as valuable as Qarlo—grabbed him, and *did* somehow manage to work out the concepts behind the rifle, the firmer, the mono-atomic anti-gravity device in the pouch? What then? (3) A man used to war, knowing only war, would eventually *seek* or foment war.

There were dozens of others, they were only beginning to realize. No, something had to be done with him.

Imprison him?

For what? The man had done no real harm. He had not intentionally caused the death of the man on the subway platform. He had been frightened by the train. He had been attacked by the executives—one of whom had a broken neck, but was alive. No, he was just "a stranger and afraid, in a world I never made," as Housman had put it so terrifyingly clearly.

Kill him?

For the same reasons, unjust and brutal . . . not to mention wasteful.

Find a place for him in society?

Doing what?

Sims raged in his mind, mulled it over and tried every angle. It was an insoluble problem. A simple dogface, with no other life than that of a professional soldier, what good was he?

All Qarlo knew was war.

The question abruptly answered itself: If he knows no other life than that of a soldier . . . why, make him a soldier. (But . . . who was to say that with his knowledge of futuristic tactics and weapons, he might not turn into another Hitler, or Genghis Khan?) No, making him a soldier would only heighten the problem. There would be no peace of mind were he in a position where he might organize.

As a tactician then?

It might work at that.

Sims slumped behind his desk, pressed down the key of his intercom, spoke to the secretary, "Get me General Mainwaring, General Polk and the Secretary of Defense."

He clicked the key back. It just might work at that. If Qarlo could be persuaded to detail fighting plans, now that he realized where he was, and that the men who held him were not his enemies, and allies of Ruskie-Chink (and what a field of speculation that pair of words opened!)

It just might work . . .

. . . but Sims doubted it.

~~~~~~~~~~~~~~~

Mainwaring stayed on to report when Polk and the Secretary of Defense went back to their regular duties. He was a big man, with softness written across his face and body, and a pompous white moustache. He shook his head sadly, as though the Rosetta Stone had been stolen from him just before an all-important experiment.

"Sorry, Sims, but the man is useless to us. Brilliant grasp of military tactics, so long as it involves what he calls 'eighty-thread beams' and telepathic contacts.

"Do you know those wars up there are fought as much mentally as they are physically? Never heard of a tank or a mortar, but the stories he tells of brain-burning and spore-death would make you sick. It isn't pretty the way they fight.

"I thank God I'm not going to be around to see it; I thought *our* wars were filthy and unpleasant. They've got us licked all down the line for brutality and mass death. And the strange thing is, this Qarlo fellow *despises* it! For a while there—felt foolish as hell—but for a while there, when he was explaining it, I almost wanted to chuck my career, go out and start beating the drum for disarmament."

The General summed up, and it was apparent Qarlo was useless as a tactician. He had been brought up with one way of waging war, and it would take a lifetime for him to adjust enough to be of any tactical use.

But it didn't really matter, for Sims was certain the General had given him the answer to the problem, inadvertently.

He would have to clear it with Security, and the President, of course. And it would take a great deal of publicity to make the people realize this man actually *was* the real thing, an inhabitant of the future. But if it worked out, Qarlo Clobregnny, the soldier and nothing *but* the soldier, could be the most valuable man Time had ever spawned.

He set to work on it, wondering foolishly if he wasn't too much the idealist.

~~~~~~~~~~~~~~~~

Ten soldiers crouched in the frozen mud. Their firmers had been jammed, had turned the sand and dirt of their holes only to icelike conditions. The cold was seeping up through their suits, and the jammed firmers were emitting hard radiation. One of the men screamed as the radiation took hold in his gut, and he felt the organs watering away. He leaped up, vomiting blood and phlegm—and was caught across the face by a robot-tracked triple beam. The front of his face disappeared, and the nearly decapitated corpse flopped back into the firmhole, atop a comrade.

That soldier shoved the body aside carelessly, thinking of his four children, lost to him forever in a Ruskie-Chink raid on Garmatopolis, sent to the bogs to work. His mind conjured up the sight of the three girls and the little boy with such long, long eyelashes—each dragging through the stinking bog, a mineral bag tied to the neck, collecting fuel rocks for the enemy. He began to cry softly. The sound and mental image of crying was picked up by a Ruskie-Chink telepath somewhere across the lines, and even before the man could catch himself, blank his mind, the telepath was on him.

The soldier raised up from the firmhole bottom, clutching with crooked hands at his head. He began to tear at his features wildly, screaming high and piercing, as the enemy telepath burned away his brain. In a moment his eyes were empty, staring shells, and the man flopped down beside his comrade, who had begun to deteriorate.

A thirty-eight thread whined its beam overhead, and the eight remaining men saw a munitions wheel go up with a deafening roar. Hot shrapnel zoomed across the field, and a thin, brittle, knife-edged bit of plasteel arced over the edge of the firmhole, and buried itself in one soldier's head. The piece went in crookedly, through his left earlobe, and came out skewering his tongue, half-extended from his open mouth. From the side it looked as though he were wearing some sort of earring. He died in spasms, and it took an awfully long while. Finally, the twitching and gulping got so bad, one of his comrades used the butt of a Brandelmeier across the dying man's nose. It splintered the nose, sent bone chips into the brain, killing the man instantly.

Then the attack call came!

In each of their heads, the telepathic cry came to advance, and they were up out of the firmhole, all seven of them, reciting their daily prayer, and knowing it would do no good. They advanced across the slushy ground, and overhead they could hear the buzz of leech bombs, coming down on the enemy's thread emplacements.

All around them in the deep-set night the varicolored explosions popped and sugged, expanding in all directions like fireworks, then dimming the scene, again the blackness.

One of the soldiers caught a beam across the belly, and he was thrown sidewise for ten feet, to land in a soggy heap, his stomach split open, the organs glowing and pulsing wetly from the charge of the threader. A head popped out of a firmhole before them, and three of the remaining six fired simultaneously. The enemy was a booby—rigged to backtrack their kill urge, rigged to a telepathic hookup—and even as the body exploded under their combined firepower, each of the men caught fire. Flames leaped from their mouths, from their pores, from the instantly charred spaces where their eyes had been. A pyrotic-telepath had been at work.

The remaining three split and cut away, realizing they might be thinking, might be giving themselves away. That was the horror of being just a dogface, not a special telepath behind the lines. Out here . . . nothing but death.

A doggie-mine slithered across the ground, entwined itself in the legs of one soldier, and blew the legs out from under him. He lay there clutching the shredded stumps, feeling the blood soaking into the mud, and then unconsciousness seeped into his brain. He died shortly thereafter.

Of the two left, one leaped a barbwall, and blasted out a thirty-eight thread emplacement of twelve men, at the cost of the top of his head. He was left alive, and curiously, as though the war had stopped, he felt the top of himself, and his fingers pressed lightly against convoluted, slick matter for a second before he dropped to the ground.

His braincase was open, glowed strangely in the night, but no one saw it.

The last soldier dove under a beam that zzzzzzzed through the night, and landed on his elbows. He rolled with the tumble, felt the edge of a leech-bomb crater, and dove in headfirst. The beam split up his passage, and he escaped charring by an inch. He lay in the hollow, feeling the cold of the battlefield seeping around him, and drew his cloak closer.

The soldier was Qarlo . . .

He finished talking, and sat down on the platform …

The audience was silent . . .

Sims shrugged into his coat, fished around in the pocket for the cold pipe. The dottle had fallen out of the bowl, and he felt the dark grains at the bottom of the pocket. The audience was filing out slowly, hardly anyone speaking, but each staring at others around him. As though they were suddenly realizing what had happened to them, as though they were looking for a solution.

Sims passed such a solution. The petitions were there, tacked up alongside the big sign—duplicate of the ones up all over the city. He caught the heavy black type on them as he passed through the auditorium's vestibule:

SIGN THIS PETITION!
PREVENT WHAT YOU HAVE HEARD TONIGHT!

People were flocking around the petitions, but Sims knew it was only a token gesture at this point: the legislation had gone through that morning. No more war . . . under any conditions. And intelligence reported the long playing records, the piped broadcasts, the p.a. trucks, had all done their jobs. Similar legislation was going through all over the world.

It looked as though Qarlo had done it, single-handed.

Sims stopped to refill his pipe, and stared up at the big black-lined poster near the door.

> HEAR QARLO, THE SOLDIER FROM THE FUTURE!
> SEE THE MAN FROM TOMORROW,
> AND HEAR HIS STORIES OF THE WONDERFUL
> WORLD OF THE FUTURE!
> FREE! NO OBLIGATIONS! HURRY!

The advertising had been effective, and it was a fine campaign.

Qarlo had been more valuable just telling about his Wars, about how men died in that day in the future, than he ever could have been as a strategist.

It took a real soldier, who hated war, to talk of it, to show people that it was ugly, and unglamorous. And there was a certain sense of foul defeat, of hopelessness, in knowing the future was the way Qarlo described it. It made you want to stop the flow of Time, say, "No. The future will *not* be like this! We will abolish war!"

Certainly enough steps in the right direction had been taken. The legislature was there, and those who had held back, who had tried to keep animosity alive, were being disposed of every day.

Qarlo had done his work well.

There was just one thing bothering special advisor Lyle Sims. The soldier had come back in time, so he was here. That much they knew for certain.

But a nagging worry ate at Sims's mind, made him say prayers he had thought himself incapable of inventing. Made him fight to get Qarlo heard by everyone …

Could the future be changed?
Or was it inevitable?
Would Qarlo's world inevitably come 'round?
Would all their work be for nothing?
It couldn't be! It dare not be.
He walked back inside, got in line to sign the petitions again, though it was his fiftieth time.

~~~~~~~~~~~~

HARLAN ELLISON changes whatever he touches. He has changed the field of science fiction, changed the face of horror fiction, changed the shape of contemporary fiction, changed how an entire generation looks at movies and television, changed all of us who have come into contact with his work.

Whether you first met the early stories of street gangs and turf wars (Gentleman Junkie, for example), or the incomparable science fiction short stories ("I Have No Mouth and I Must Scream," "A Boy and His Dog," "Jeffty Is Five," and hundreds more), or the essays about the boob tube collected as The Glass Teat *and* The Other Glass Teat, *or whether you read his landmark anthologies* Dangerous Visions *and* Again, Dangerous Visions, *or whether you've been lucky enough to hear the man speak (who says the preachers are the only great orators we have left?), you know that Ellison has two qualities almost never found together in this world: first, he's a tough guy who doesn't take crap, doesn't suffer fools and doesn't blink twice when he sees how ugly things can get; second, he's got one of the softest hearts and the warmest, most caring personalities you'll ever meet.*

Hard edges and compassion don't often come in the same package. When they do, and when they're laced with an extraordinary dollop of writing talent, there's only one thing to do—read every word the man writes.

Ellison lives in Sherman Oaks, California, with his wife Susan. He has received seven Hugo Awards (given by the readers) and three Nebula Awards (given by the writers). His collected works are being reissued by White Wolf Publishing, beginning with Edgeworks *(now available).*

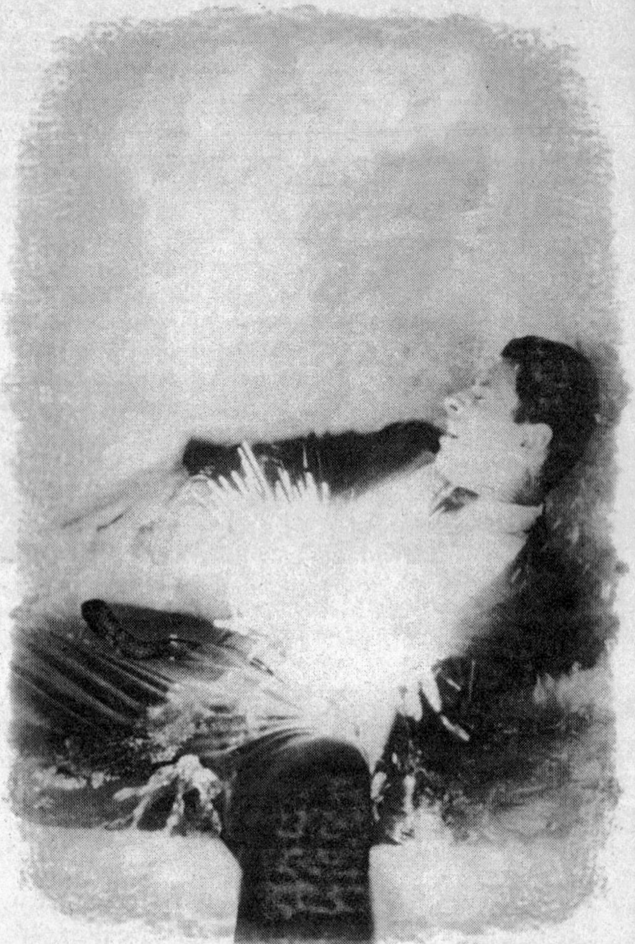

The line that divides science from the supernatural is often blurred and indistinct. We look at centuries-old carvings in stone and wonder if the beings depicted there are gods, demons, or ancient astronauts. Like the fairy circles of folklore, crop circles appear overnight and we speculate that they may be messages from the stars. In old books we read of elder races and cosmic destroyers, and we wonder . . .

The will to power is a constant factor in human interactions; and there are always those among us who seek the ultimate—control over life and death. In this adaptation of an Outer Limits *classic, a scientist discovers the dangerous lure of exploration at the edge of the unknowable when it offers the possibility of limitless power.*

It Crawled out of the Woodwork

Adaptation by Diane Duane
Original Screenplay by Joseph Stefano

THE SAN FERNANDO VALLEY shares the reputation of the rest of the Los Angeles area for relatively good weather. Not that conditions there are perfect. The occasional earthquake has been known to mar the mood—not surprising, when you consider the fifty blind-thrust faults littering the place. And there are flash floods sometimes in the spring and fall, but even those are mostly controlled, the Valley being, after all, part of "the place where they pave the rivers."

The thunderstorm weather, though, can catch you by surprise sometimes. Mostly in the spring, those big thundercloud-fringed weather fronts come rolling down from the Angeles Mountains, and over the northern barrier of hills, Oat Mountain and its neighbors. Those storms come racketing down into the Valley, the thunder echoing from hill to hill until it sounds like the end of the world, and the rain comes bucketing down so that you can hardly see ten feet ahead of you.

This was one of those nights. Down nearer the Valley floor, the main drag, Reseda Boulevard, was rapidly becoming the Reseda River: parked cars were up to their wheel-arches in water, and the parking lots on either side of the boulevard were beginning to look as if they should be stocked with trout. Houses on the rising ground in the north Valley, up past San Fernando Mission Boulevard near Porter Ranch, were losing the topsoil and new plantings in their back yards; the mud and the sapling conifers would probably be found, in the morning, somewhere down in Tarzana.

In the hills, the water was busy turning creases into gullies, and gullies into little down-roaring waterfalls of muddy water, everywhere except on those hillsides where the manzanita and the palm had been planted close enough to keep the downflow from carrying everything away with it.

Up on one of those hillsides, the rain came lashing down onto an extensive walled compound: iron-gated, a bleak-looking place in the near-continuous flashes of lightning and the shriek of the wind. Every now and then the smell of ozone got strong enough to cause coughing, and hair would stand on end as lightning danced about or hit one of the big microwave transmission towers up on the crest of Oat Mountain.

Just in the shadow of the crest, under the tower, the compound stood.

If you walked up to the gate, which not many did—first of all because it was remote, and, second, because very few people knew the place was there—you would see, in the lightning flashes and the occasionally uncertain flickering of the lamps by the gate, a sign with the letters NORCO, and underneath this in smaller letters, ENERGY RESEARCH COMMISSION, SAN FERNANDO VALLEY DIVISION. All very plain, very institutional looking: there was nothing much to give away what kind of institution might be involved. Private? Public? Either way, it was the kind of place that made you think, looking at it, that such questions were probably better left unasked. Certainly it was far enough away from the more frequented parts of the Valley that few people were likely to stumble on it by accident.

Inside the main lab at Norco, Rosa Estes was going about her nightly business. Rosa was a small dark woman, plainly dressed, as suited her work: her paychecks, cut by computers at one or another accountancy firm, said "domestic engineer," but she laughed at the name: she was a cleaning lady. Norco was usually her third stop, after doing a few doctors' and lawyers' offices down at Reseda and Woodman. She hated the drive up here, on a road that was surprisingly bad by Valley standards, and not good even if the place had been up in the Angeles National Forest. It was mostly a rutted, stony track that turned into a rutted, stony river in this weather, and it wasn't paved until practically in front of the gates. She had had to replace her shocks twice in a two-year period, and she was beginning to think about charging Norco for having (inevitably) to wash the car after every thrice-weekly visit. All the same, they paid well, which was something when you had three kids to support, and the mortgage your no-good-bum husband had left you to service by yourself.

Outside, the freakish thunder banged and the lightning flickered like a power outage waiting to happen. Rosa half wished that it would. She'd have an excuse to go home early, then. But no such luck. She got the ancient canister vacuum cleaner out of its closet, hauled it over to the wall, and plugged it in, wondering, as usual, why they couldn't get something better. The vacuum was of a superannuated industrial type that looked like a giant baked bean can, and had, in Rosa's opinion, suction that was about as effective. The company might pay well, but they saw no particular need to replace something as prosaic as janitorial equipment that worked fine—or, at least worked, however it coughed and spluttered. They were too busy spending money on—

She glanced around the room at the desks covered with incomprehensible equipment: computers, and objects much less identifiable, all of which sat humming and chuckling to themselves, and all of which attracted a terrific amount of dust. *Cheapskates,* Rosa

It Crawled out of the Woodwork   41

thought. *Eighty thousand bucks' worth of computers in here, probably, but can they buy me something that wasn't first used in the Stone Age? Of course not. And what do they do with all this stuff all day? Probably play games and send other scientists dirty e-mails* . . . She sighed, and went back to her vacuuming.

Her back complained, as it usually did. For the ten thousandth time she considered giving this work up. *For what? Doing the paper-or-plastic routine in Gelson's?* She had no other job skills. And her clientele were okay, really: she didn't have to clean any disgusting places, not like poor 'Smerelda down the street, who couldn't get anyplace better to do than the police station, and had to drive right over to the west Valley for even that . . . .

Her back twinged her again, sharply. Rosa did her best to ignore it as she worked her way over into one of the corners. There was a lump of fluff down there by the baseboard: sooty-looking stuff. She shoved the vacuum head at it, but the head was the wrong shape and size to get into the corner effectively. *Cheapskates . . . and the suction on this thing is so bad anyway.* Sighing, Rosa picked up the vacuum hose, pulled the head off—it would probably work better without it anyway—and attacked the lump of fluff again.

It remained stubbornly stuck in the corner. *What do they do,* she thought, *glue these things down? All these fancy scientists running around in their white coats, how can they be so messy?* Rosa bent down with a cleaning rag and pulled at the thing. It seemed to be snagged on the baseboard somehow; or maybe there was some more of it stuck back there.

Boy, she thought, *this better not be anything dangerous. Asbestos or something.* It was always a worry in these big factory kind of places. But then, she had never seen anything here that looked dangerous, any chemicals or stuff like that . . . . And Rosa was in a good position to know the company's secrets: there wasn't a closet or storeroom at Norco that she didn't know the contents of.

The fuzzy object seemed to give a little bit as she pulled. She made a thoughtful face, and went at it again with the vacuum hose.

Slowly, a little recalcitrantly, the fuzzball started to go up the hose. The vacuum began to wheeze and whine on a higher note, complaining. Then abruptly the dust bunny let go its grip on the baseboard and went up the tube. Rosa rolled her eyes a little at the noise it made as it went up: that godawful sucking sound. *Don't let it get stuck,* she thought. *Just what I'd need tonight . . .*

The sucking sound persisted, and got louder as the fluff went up the hose, and then into the vacuum. There was the expected faint "hup!" noise as the vacuum ingested the fluff-lump. Rosa waited for the sound of the vacuum starting to suck normally again. But the sound didn't come. *Dumb thing, you're gonna break on me now, huh? . . . That's it. Tomorrow morning I leave them a note and tell them, get a new vacuum or get a new domestic engineer.*

She turned. Her eyes widened. The canister of the vacuum was swelling, like a can of baked beans that had not only gone bad, but was getting worse while she watched. It swelled and bulged, making a horrendous groaning noise, and after a moment, the top of the vacuum blew right off.

Rosa flinched—and then her mouth fell open at the sight of what came out. Something that moaned, making the same wheezing, shrieking noise that the vacuum hose had been making, but with another sound wound through it, a kind of moaning thunder, like the thunder outside. And it flickered, too, a kind of spasmodic cloud-shape, with lightning strobing inside it, like the lightning outside. That cloud rose up out of the canister, writhed, roiled, reached out to her—

Rosa, backed up against the wall, had nowhere to go. She flung her hand in front of her face to shield herself from the light, strobe-bright, getting brighter, and flashing down into that awful, hot, hungry dark again. The cloud-shape reached out to her, flung itself around her, pierced her through with lightning bolts. Her scream and its scream, became one, indissoluble, as it grew. The whole roomful of desks and blinking machinery flickered with the blazing of its lightning, bright and dark, and hungry; hungry for more . . .

~~~~~~~~~~~~~~~~

The Valley being where it is, the bad weather never lasts long. Any number of sunlit mornings later, the paved area around the front gate at Norco looked as it usually did: very clean, very arid, with a guard sitting outside on a very institutional metal chair, in the deadly quiet.

His name was Warren Edgar Morley. For the past six months, he had guarded this gate from eight in the morning until six at night—at which time he was replaced by another just like himself.

But not today.

Morley reached into his pocket, pulled out a pack of cigarettes and a matchbook, and struck a light. He knew he shouldn't really be smoking: but he simply hadn't been able to quit after the operation, no matter what the doctor said. It was partly just the old habit, and partly his nerves . . . which had gotten a lot worse after the operation. He had never been the same after the heart attack, no matter what the doctor said to cheer him up. At least he hadn't lost his job, but in retrospect, he wondered if maybe it would have been better if he had . . .

From down the bad road, then, he heard a car coming up: it was just swinging past the chain-link fence that protected the side of the place, and into the open area in front of the gate.

Morley dropped the match as the light-colored sedan pulled up to the gate. He chucked the cigarette, and stood up with his hand on his gun. There were two men in the car, both dark-haired and relatively young; the driver, a little taller than the passenger, sober-faced; the passenger a little younger, curly-haired, with a casual but cheerful expression.

As Morley walked up to the car, the younger one

said in an amused voice, "Hey, Stu, the kids ain't friendly on this block! Let's not move in."

They watched Morley calmly enough as he walked up, leaned on the driver's side window, and gave the usual litany. "Name, address, positive identification," he said, "reason for loitering outside of Norco . . . ?"

The driver smiled and said, "I'm Stuart Peters . . ."

"*Professor* Stuart Peters," said the younger man, a little pointedly, a little proudly.

"I begin working here tomorrow morning," the driver said to Morley. "We drove clear across the country, my brother and I."

The younger man, the brother, laughed. "We haven't even found a place to live yet. The professor couldn't wait to get a look at . . . that!"

Morley looked at them both for a moment: the look they gave him back was so calm and open that he figured they had to be telling the truth. "Okay," he said at last, letting his gun ease back into its normal place in the holster. "But look fast. Nobody's allowed to hang around here."

They nodded as he stepped away from the car and headed back to the gate. For a moment he paused, looking at the matchbook that he still held in his other hand.

I wonder, could I just let them know . . . No, better not. What if the doctor finds out . . . For he found things out, sometimes, that you weren't sure how he knew. There was always the possibility that there were cameras hidden around here, security cameras that not even the staff knew about. The place was full of secrets: eight months working here, and he still wasn't sure who owned Norco, or what they did here. The government? Some big company, doing research on the quiet? No telling.

Still. This could be the chance—

He reached into the inside pocket of his jacket for a pencil, and hurriedly scribbled inside the cover of the matchbook.

Behind him, the engine of the car started up again. Morley turned hurriedly, and ran back toward the car. "Hey!"

The car paused: the two men inside looked at him a little quizzically. Morley said, "You have a cigarette?"

The younger man felt around in his breast pocket for a moment, then came up with a soft pack of cigarettes and handed them to Morley. Morley tapped one out, struck a match from his matchbook, lit the cigarette hurriedly. Then he handed the matchbook and the cigarette pack back to the young passenger, who pocketed them.

They K-turned and drove back down the way they came. Slowly Morley walked back toward the gate. *There's a chance, then,* he thought. *Just a chance. Why should what happened to me, happen to him? If he has any sense . . . if he'll just believe it, and not think it's some crackpot stunt . . .*

As the car behind him swung around the curve and out of sight, the wind began to rise. Morley looked up, and his eyes widened, and his mouth gaped, stretched out of shape in fear. He clutched at his chest, and started gasping, wheezing for breath.

Inside the gate, something dark and bright, like

lightning in broad daylight, like a black cloud with white fire wrapped up in it, came hastening down the path, heading for him with a roar like wind and thunder. He had only seen it once before, and he had never wanted to see it again . . . but that hope was now vain. Collapsing to his knees, Warren Edgar Morley cried, "No, please! I didn't say anything! I didn't! Please! No!"

It didn't care, any more than it had the first time he saw it, when the world had gone black with fear, when the breath had stopped in his body and he had been cold as ice, trapped in the blackness (as he then thought) forever. When he woke up, after what seemed much more than just one eternity, he had found a little ticking box strapped to his chest, and the doctor's face looking down on him with a strange cool expression of concern oddly mixed with a bizarre pleasure. Now, though, the doctor was nowhere near . . . though he might be watching. "No!" Morley screamed one last time, desperate.

The roiling cloud of fire and darkness came pouring through the gate, unstoppable as a storm, and wreathed itself around Morley in a garment of thunder. When it finally backed away, the man was gone. The cloud roared back up the path again, a stain in the bright sunshine, and took itself away out of sight.

~~~~~~~~~~

The motel was one of the more salubrious ones on Devonshire Street in Northridge, which meant that the decor was no worse than late-fifties painted concrete, with brick facings everywhere there wasn't paint. Inside one of the downstairs rooms, the passenger Morley had given the matchbook to lay on the bed, toying absently with the chenille of the cheap bedspread, and talking on the phone.

"Is this Gaby Christian? You don't know me, and you probably have a dinner date anyway, but we have a mutual friend in Kingston, New York, whose name is of no importance here—"

His taller brother came ambling out of the bathroom, adjusting his shirt-cuffs and looking a little quizzically at Jory, who was talking with the speed and confidence of a used-car salesman. "—and he suggested I call you the minute I arrived in LA.— Harvey Miller. He went to school with your brother."

Stuart Peters sat down at the desk, intent on not hearing yet another of his brother's outrageous flights of fantasy, especially since it was more than likely to be successful. He glanced at the assorted paperwork that covered the desk: mostly excerpted scientific papers that he had sworn he would get caught up on, and torn-out notebook pages covered with his tidy script. He had a lot of catching up to do, both on papers he was writing for his research, some of them getting dangerously close to deadline, and the ones he was writing for pleasure: excursions down byroads of physics that were either (at the moment) wildly unpopular, like questioning the "thought-experiment" style of scientific method as applied to relativity, or scholia which were simply wildly unlikely, such as the paper presently entitled "Taub-NUT Space as an Answer to

Practically Everything."

Stuart had a quixotic streak, always a slightly dangerous trait for a physicist, worse in times like these. A wave of conservatism was beginning to spread across the field, and he heartily hoped he would live long enough to see the tide go out again. Meanwhile, he wrote papers which he knew could not be published for years, until the field had loosened up a little: and in places where it was loose already, he did what work he could. That was why he was here, sitting in a motel room which had apparently been decorated by someone who had been Torquemada in a previous life—judging both by the comfort of the furniture, and the print on the curtains.

Stuart started turning the pages over, looking for his cigarettes: found them, and then started pulling open desk drawers, looking for a match. He found stationery, some of the sheets featuring what appeared to be old red wine stains—fortunately the wrong color for blood—several worn-down and enthusiastically chewed pencils, and a Gideon Bible, but no matches. Finally he turned to look at his brother, snapped his fingers a couple of times to get his attention, and pointed at the cigarette in his mouth.

"I'm not as young as I sound, Miss Christian, and anyway, I *think* old," his brother said cheerfully, feeling around in his shirt pocket and coming up with a matchbook. "—No, but only because I haven't met the right girl yet." He tossed the matchbook to Stuart at the desk. "I will be most happy to marry you, Miss Christian. If it turns out you're the right girl, we will marry in haste. Meanwhile, shall we repent in advance? Over a leisurely dinner?"

Stuart raised his eyebrows in the old familiar bemusement. His brother and women . . . any woman . . . . What always amazed Stuart, who was more reticent of nature than Jory, was that the women actually seemed to *like* these hilarious come-ons, at least when it was Jory producing them.

Marriage, though? he thought. *Not likely.*

It was one of the few slightly uncomfortable aspects of his life: he loved his brother, and his brother loved him, and they were nearly inseparable. The problem was that the inseparability was mostly on Jory's side, and Stuart had no clear idea, as yet, how to break him of it. Nonetheless, Jory played the field with great energy and skill, and as a result, embarrassing numbers of women followed him around with their own versions of inseparability. There had been some uncomfortable scenes just before they left Kingston, most of which Stuart thanked the gods of physics he had not had to witness himself.

In the background, the sweet-talking went on. Shaking his head, Stuart smiled slightly as he pulled out a match and struck it; then did a double take, glancing at the inside of the matchbook, as he lit the cigarette. Inside it, scribbled hastily in pencil, were the words, DON'T COME BACK NORCO DOOMED.

Now what the hell—

"Right," Jory was saying cheerfully. "Eight-thirty at the Trasteveria Coffee House." He paused, his eyebrows up. "Yes, I know what you look like. I've seen all your TV shows. —Oh, you'll recognize me. I'll be wearing *you* in my eyes." He rolled over and hung up, looking immensely satisfied.

TV shows? . . . Stuart wondered. But something more immediate was on his mind. He rose from the desk, still looking at the matchbook, and went over to the bed. Joey eyed him with mild apprehension, getting up.

"All right, what'd I do now?"

It was very much the little-brother-in-trouble voice, which for the moment Stuart ignored. He showed Jory the matchbook. "Where'd you get these?"

Jory blinked. "Are they mine?"

"You took them out of your pocket and threw them at me."

Stuart handed the matchbook back to Jory. Jory gazed at it thoughtfully, with no sign of recognition. "They're not mine."

Stuart rolled his eyes. "Think hard."

"Okay. —I know—that guard gave them to me."

"Read the inside."

Jory read it. "'Norco doomed!'" He handed the matchbook back, laughing, and made his way to the chair by the bathroom door, where his jacket was hanging. "Must've been meant for *you*, since I'd marry Miss Christian before I'd be caught dead working in a place like Norco."

Stuart made a wry face as his brother shrugged into his jacket. He had heard this before. Jory had not been wild about the upsetting of their comfortable and settled life back in New York for the sake of a cross-country trek ending in some weird job out in

Los Angeles—a place known to all New Yorkers, especially the upstate variety, as the very epicenter of kooks, weirdos, and nutcases. Now Jory straightened his tie, and said, in a voice that suggested he was now ready to discuss *really* serious things, "You know what's worrying me, Stu?"

"No, Jory, what's worrying you?"

"Gaby Christian." Jory said, giving himself a last long look in the mirror. "I never told her my name. She's having dinner with a man she's never seen before, and she didn't even remind me to tell her my name."

Stuart thought that this was par for the course for nearly any woman who had suddenly run into Jory, even over the phone, for the first time. *'Christian'. . . TV . . .? Oh. The actress. Now where did he get her phone number?*

Never mind that. He'll be trying to sucker you into going along as a chaperon, next.

But, to Stuart's relief, this was apparently not in the cards. Jory headed for the door. ". . . Mind if I stay out late?" Jory said, pausing just long enough to double-check his tie in the mirror and re-straighten it minutely.

"No," Stuart said, still gazing in some bemusement at the matchbook cover. The handwriting was hasty, but not particularly disturbed-looking. *Not my area of expertise, though. It'd be just my luck to be holding the scribblings of a madman who'd been winning penmanship contests since he was six.*

"All night?" Jory said.
"Of course," Stuart said, still somewhat distracted.
"Hah! Some brother's keeper you are."
Stuart folded the matchbook cover down again, turned it over in his hands as the door opened, briefly letting in the light of the streetlights out in the parking lot.

It was sunlight that shone next on that matchbook, falling on it through big windows as it was turned over in another pair of hands. Dr. Block looked up from the desk in his office, having folded down the cover of the matchbook again, to hide its message.

"One of *our* guards gave you this?" He said it in a bemused way, and in an accent that spoke of central Europe: Leipzig, if Stuart remembered correctly, and then Dresden, where Block had done postwar work on quark pairings and heavy-electron shell anomalies. His voice was soft and understated, rather dry, like its owner. Block was a tall, iron-haired, iron-eyed man in a dead black suit, who carried about him a sense of great restraint, a great deal that he could say, and didn't. Probably the effect came of all those years spent in parts of the world where even physics was thoroughly politicized, and your opinions on the uses of deuterium or helium-neon lasers could get a medal pinned on you, or get you shot, depending on who you told and what you told them. Probably his name had been spelled Bloch once, but enough people (without logical reason) would have questioned his loyalty if he had kept it. If Block looked like anything to Stuart, he looked like an utter pragmatist.

Now Block eyed Stuart Peters with a cool expression: restrained still, but with a suggestion that there were limits to the restraint, limits beyond which it might not be wise to press. And jokes, especially at this early date, would be pushing those limits.

"Yes, sir," Stuart said. "The guard at the main gate."

Block immediately leaned over to his intercom. "Miss Seltzer, get me the main gate."

"A different man is there today," Stuart said.

Block glanced at him, made a slight moue of acknowledgment. "Never mind, Miss Seltzer," he said, and clicked off the intercom again.

While this was going on, Stuart gazed up at the framed photograph hanging on the wall behind Dr. Block, controlling a brief burst of curiosity about the aesthetic sense of anyone who would hang a photo of a nuclear explosion on the wall above his desk. Or was it some kind of message, perhaps? A statement about some hidden attitude to war, or peace, or energy? A warning about the temper of the office's occupant? An attempt to butter up some visiting fund-allocator from the DOD? But doubtless he would find out eventually . . . .

Block was looking at him again. "Yesterday's guard was older," Stuart said.

Block nodded, leaned back in his chair with a look

that might have been approval of a new man's acuteness of observation . . . *might* have.

"We have a problem here at Norco, Doctor Peters," Block said. "As a matter of fact, we are slaves to it." His tone of voice was not entirely one of dissatisfaction with the slavery, Stuart noticed.

Block said, "We accepted your application—the first one we've accepted in six months, incidentally—because we believe only a new fresh-minded physicist will be able to help us with our problem. I'm very glad you didn't take this message seriously."

Stuart blinked, and didn't respond, at least not overtly, to the flattery. He had heard this kind of thing before: and among scientists of a certain stripe, "fresh-minded" could be taken several different ways. "I didn't say that," Stuart said.

"And yet here you are, bright and early, on the job."

Stuart made a so-what expression: Block's initial sharp reaction, followed by this bland put-off, made him slightly uncomfortable: made him wonder if somehow he was being tested. *Or maybe it's just irrational paranoia on my part. Still . . .* "Will you talk to the guard who was on duty yesterday?" Stuart said.

Block leaned back in his seat again and glanced down at some papers on the desk—not really referring to them, Stuart thought, but giving himself a moment to change tracks. Stuart restrained himself from smiling: this was the reason a lot of senior academics he knew took to smoking pipes, specifically pipes which never stayed lit and required constant attention and long pauses while dealing with them. "In your application," Block said, "you stated that you were not married and had no other dependents."

"That's right."

"Yet you came west with . . . you said a younger brother?"

Stuart nodded. *I wondered if this was going to start being a problem . . . Damn.* "I didn't plan to have him come along," he said, as lightly as seemed appropriate when discussing a family matter with a stranger. "As a matter of fact, I thought my moving would be . . . good for him. But . . . he doesn't like being on his own. He dropped out of school to remain with me."

Block frowned. "How old is he?"

"Twenty." Stuart gestured casually. "I couldn't refuse, or make him stay behind. We have no parents or other relatives."

Block continued to look somewhat concerned. "Is he given to practical joking?"

Stuart put up an eyebrow in surprise. *But then I probably should have anticipated this line of inquiry—* "As a matter of fact . . . his humor is fairly mature. A scary note scribbled on a matchbook wouldn't be his style . . . if that's what you're thinking."

Block looked away, reached down to put the matchbook away in a drawer, and rose. "You're to report to Professor Linden."

"So I hear."

He led Stuart toward the door. "I arranged that myself," said Dr. Block. "The Professor could use *someone with a fresh approach."*

Stuart wondered what *that* meant. Was he going to be stuck with some old theoretical fogy who wouldn't know a new idea if one bit him, and wouldn't like one even if it didn't bite? He thought, as he often had over the last few years, of the line attributed (though possibly erroneously) to Einstein, an answer to the question of what to do when confronted with a world full of old scientists who wouldn't accept new theories, or worse, the theories' confirmation: "You wait for the old scientists to die."

Now as then, Stuart wondered about the quote's attribution: it sounded little like the affable genius which was generally Einstein's public face. But even Einstein must have gotten cranky occasionally . . . . and Stuart had gotten cranky, and found himself waiting for old scientists to die, a lot more often than that. He could not understand how anyone could refuse to acknowledge the truth just out of stubbornness, or being set in their habits of thinking or worldview. Please, he said to whatever power was behind physics, not another one I'll have to wait for . . .

As he and Block headed out into the corridor together, Stuart threw a last glance over his shoulder at the photo of the atomic explosion, frozen into eternal sedateness behind its glass, and raised his eyebrows again. It was strange—but any new place was going to seem strange on the first day, matchbooks or no matchbooks . . .

The main laboratory was full of the sound of suppressed power; dynamos running somewhere, computers and other machinery ticking over quietly. Apparently tending the machines and checking the computers, moving quietly from one piece of equipment to the next, was a handsome woman with blonde hair cut tidily just above the shoulders, wearing a modest checked shirtdress and a cool expression.

As she examined the readout on the front panel of one of the machines, a buzzer sounded. The woman left the piece of equipment, walked over to a wall panel, touched a button on it. "Hello?"

"Dr. Block is bringing the new man," said one of the guards' voices.

The woman left the panel and moved slowly over to a nearby coat rack, removing from a coat hanger a white lab coat. She started buttoning up the front, deliberately but without haste. Her fingers lingered for a moment over the buttons just at her waist, where, attached to a black belt which did not match the shirtdress, a small oblong metal box was strapped, a box with two dials and a pair of small lights. She carefully buttoned the lab coat over it, not looking at the box, as if unwilling to do so.

The laboratory door opened, and Dr. Block and the new man came in. Block headed over toward her, with the stranger in tow. "Professor Linden?" Block said, cheerfully enough.

The woman turned slowly. Stuart, standing near the door, couldn't yet see her face; but the effect was of someone either too tired to move quickly, or of someone unwilling to hurry at the sound of a voice she knew too well, and possibly disliked. She was handsome, very handsome indeed: but her face and her eyes were so tired . . .

For all her good looks, Jory wouldn't waste his time on this one, Stuart thought: *she's got an extra twenty years in her eyes.* Then he felt embarrassed at the thought. But it was shocking, the age he saw in that smooth face. *Like someone who's seen a lot of pain, or ...*

She turned, then, and came to meet them, deliberately but with grace. "Your new collaborator," Block said, "Professor Stuart Peters."

Stuart held out his hand, but for the moment the woman was distracted, looking at Block with an expression on her face that looked like more than mere dislike. After a moment Stuart let his hand drop, rather than stand there holding it out like a wet fish. Block, as if noting none of this, said cheerfully, "I told him we were slaves to a problem of grotesque proportions, Stephanie. But nothing more. Just enough to whet his appetite."

"Oh. I see." She gave Stuart a small formal bow, very restrained indeed. "Welcome."

Stuart smiled, but again, the Professor didn't see it. She was looking at Block, as if waiting for a lead to follow. Her face was very still, very controlled—a different kind of control from Block's.

"Show him about a bit, Stephanie," Block said, "and tell him the rules. Strict rules," he said in Stuart's direction, "don't sound so strict when they come from the lips of a beautiful woman."

Stuart kept himself from frowning at the slight nudge-nudge-wink-wink tone of Block's voice. *Did he catch me staring at her? Worse, did she?* But now Professor Linden gave Block a look suggesting strongly that she had heard all this before, and was bored with it . . . or that something else entirely was going on, something he didn't understand in the slightest. Block, smiling like a teacher approving of cooperative pupils, took himself away, and Professor Linden stood quite still until the door had closed behind him.

The atmosphere lightened perceptibly. Block's presence had been like a weight, like a kind of physical darkness—now the lights had come up again, or seemed to have. "You'll want a desk," Professor Linden said, and headed off toward one side of the lab.

Stuart went with her, slightly bemused by all this. "Shall I call you Professor Linden," he said, "or—"

She paused by an empty desk, looking down at it with much more interest than it deserved. "Will this be all right?"

"Yes. Fine."

Professor Linden looked up at Stuart again, then, and there was some guilt in the expression. "Forgive me, Professor Peters. I've fallen into the habit of not answering questions." She looked away, then, as if abashed.

"A victim of automation," Stuart said, with slight resignation, but thinking that this, at least, he understood. "We're all getting used to letting the computers do our answering for us."

She watched him as he said that. Her gaze was very unlike previous first examinations by other colleagues; Stuart became more confused. *She looks like she... pities me? She's sorry for me, somehow? What the heck have I gotten myself into here?...* But he put that aside for the moment.

"Well," Professor Linden said, turning to one of the machines, "shall we begin?"

He didn't move, for the moment. "Professor Linden?"

A little breath of impatience went out of her, not, Stuart thought, directed at him. "Stephanie."

"Stephanie. What is this 'grotesque' problem?"

She shrugged slightly, took a couple of steps away, as if from some problem she personally would prefer to avoid. "Dr. Block has a misplaced sense of word value. It isn't an *ordinary* problem, but..."

"But it isn't grotesque, either."

"No. Merely insoluble." She said it as if this were a personal problem for her.

Stuart nodded at this attitude—he had met it before. "They're the kind I hope to specialize in when I grow up."

Her quick glance suggested that she did not consider growing up to be a problem he needed to spend much time on. "We understood you've already created a minor stir solving the unsolvable... and making fools of foolish law-makers."

Stuart smiled very slightly: this at least was partially true, and certainly would have been a reason for his getting this job quickly. The uproar at MIT over his paper on his SLAC multiple-shell results still had not died down, causing him to be roundly condemned by most of the physicists "for" whom he was waiting. "All but one," Stuart said. "Nature."

"Perhaps because she doesn't make foolish laws." Professor Linden said it in an approving tone: then she glanced away again. "I'll show you around," she said, moving away.

He didn't move, for the moment. "Stephanie?"

She paused, looked back.

"The problem?" he prompted, as gently as he could. He had no desire to antagonize her, and increasingly he was getting the idea that she had something else on her mind.

Professor Linden gave him a challenging look. "We have to find a way to break or change the law of Conservation of Energy."

Jeez, he thought. *I wanted to go somewhere where people believed in starting at the top . . . I got my wish. I should be more careful about what I ask for in future . . .* "Oh," was all he could find to say out loud.

"You don't think we'll succeed?"

He had thought, once, that his first "real job" was likely to be fairly boring, but now it became plain that it was going to be a lot more exciting than he had suspected even in his wilder flights of speculation. "The law states that energy can be changed in form," he said, "but cannot be either created or destroyed." It was practically the basis of all modern physics, that law; the source of much frustration in many scholia. But inevitably it was taken as something that couldn't be cured, and had to be endured. He had not expected to find someone trying to do away with the source of the frustration at the root.

Professor Linden just nodded, though. "We have to find a way to create energy."

The suggestion was, on the surface anyway, so outré that Stuart dodged sidewise into humor. "It might be easier to destroy it."

"No, we've tried it. We can't." And again, Professor Linden spoke as of a most personal failure, something which had caused her much grief. That look of age showed in her face, now, most strikingly, so that Stuart found himself wanting very much to put an arm around her shoulders and tell her everything would be all right. The impulse was irrational, and he repressed it. Anyway, long experience with his brother had taught him that, no matter how many times you said it, no matter how much you wanted it to be true, only on the rarest of occasions *was* it all alright.

The phone rang: Stephanie jumped to answer it as if very relieved by the distraction. "Professor Linden here." A pause. "I'll tell him. Thank you."

She put the phone down and came back to Stuart. "You couldn't have known, of course," she said, "but one of those strict rules I'm supposed to pass on to you is in regard to phone calls. You may make none from here, and receive none."

Stuart was surprised. "Did I receive one?

"From your brother."

"Oh." Stuart laughed, just a breath. "I left a note telling him to find us an apartment. He's probably calling to tell me he's leased a ten-bedroom house . . . "

She looked at him a little sadly. "You were supposed to come alone, weren't you?"

Stuart wondered about her sorrowful expression. "I assumed that meant without wife or family."

"A brother is family."

It was the second time this subject had come up, and Stuart was beginning to get edgy, for reasons he couldn't quite pin down. And there was something about Stephanie's manner, as well: that air of lurking pain, perhaps of fear . . . "It may be first-day nerves," he said, "but I get the distinct impression that something is disturbing you. *Is* something disturbing you?"

She turned away. Normally he would have taken this as an indication to leave well enough alone, but he couldn't get rid of the feeling that a great deal might rest on his perseverance. "This is my first truly important position, Stephanie," he said. "I've looked forward to coming to Norco . . . or one of the few places like it . . . for several years. All through graduate school, all through the usual waiting years . . . Have I already done something wrong, or have I just picked the wrong place?"

She looked at him with weary eyes. There was definitely fear there . . . he was becoming more and more certain. "Physicists aren't supposed to be all that sensitive," she said.

"I'm sorry." He swallowed, abnormally conscious of his Adam's apple going up and down, and feeling more than usually adolescent. "Maybe being so near a woman is reminding me that I'm a man." Immediately after saying it, he wanted to kick himself. But the kindly, sorrowful look she gave him made him think that perhaps the comment hadn't been misconstrued, had even, perhaps, done some good. *And now that I've got the rhinoceros head, as it were, out of the middle of the room, we can talk about something else besides being young and attractive.*

"We really have to start, Professor . . . " Another kindly expression: she was letting him off the hook. Stephanie moved away from him and headed over to a panel set in the wall, beside a heavy shielded door with a small lead-glass window set in it.

He went to join her. "Stuart," he said.

She nodded, thanking him. He looked at the wall. It was an odd installation, very simplistic: a control panel set at about shoulder height, with two sets of buttons on it. There she paused, looked over her shoulder at him again. Slowly she lifted a hand to one of the buttons: pressed it. The door rolled ponderously open.

"Go ahead," she said. "I'll be with you in a minute . . . Stuart."

He stepped forward, looking at the open doorway. Beyond it was a long hallway, ending in another door. Stuart stepped through the first door, reached out to knock a tentative knuckle against the wall. It, too, was solid metal, not just lead-sheathed, apparently, but solid lead—massive. *You don't see this kind of thing except in high-energy establishments,* he thought. *You'd expect the target area of an accelerator to be on the other side of this. Power outputs in the mEv's, at least. Possibly up in the gEv's. What the devil have they got in there that needs this kind of shielding? There hasn't been anything about this kind of installation in the journals . . .*

He took a couple more steps. With a humming sound, the door behind him closed. Down at the far end of the hall, through the small window set in the opposite door, light flickered, brilliant; like lightning trapped in a box.

Stuart paused for a moment, looked through the window over his shoulder. Professor Linden was standing there, her back to the door, her head bowed. "Stephanie?" Stuart said softly, but something about the thickness of that door, the greenness of the pane of glass, told him that she couldn't hear him.

Nonetheless, he said, "Professor Linden? . . ." and knocked on the glass. She turned, but not to look at him, then moved back out of his sight.

Stuart heard the hum, but it didn't come from the door he was leaning against. It came from the one down at the end of the hall. He turned to look.

Inside that far room, he could hear a whine rising in pitch, and a sound like thunder, louder as the door opened; like a wind trapped with that thunder, stuffed into the same box, striving to get out. "Stephanie?" Stuart said again, uncertain, nervous now.

The door slid fully open. And down the hall it came, a thing like a storm cloud curdled with lightning, roaring, the wind and the thunder of it all wrapped up together. It was only imagination, surely, that made the shape seem manlike, that made it seem to have arms that reached out for him, grasping at him as it got fully out of the heavily shielded room at the end of the hall, and came gliding and roiling down the hallway toward him. The sight of it, the sound, the roar, the ozone smell, terrified him.

Stuart turned around, hammered on the door, cried, "Stephanie!" But he got no response

He had to turn, then; the roaring behind him had become too intolerable not to face. The flickering shape came charging toward him, and the howling turned from something insensate, like wind or thunder, to plain old hunger, plain old rage at being bound. And worse, to satisfaction at being fed.

He backed against the door. The darkness and the lightning overshadowed him, pierced him through. In the great and sudden silence made by the sudden absence of the sound that had always been there, the beating of his heart, he found that there was no more strength in him, no more air to breathe, no more time: and he became one with the dark . . . .

~~~~~~~~~~~~

Jory sat in the hotel room, frowning. He had been sitting that way for a long time now. His head ached a little; he wasn't clear why. And as nagging as the ache was his concern for his brother.

There was a knock at the door. He got up to answer it, paused for a moment before opening it. "Who is it?"

"A witch," whispered a voice from outside.

He opened the door. "Let me in, I think I'm being

followed," said the owner of the voice as she dashed in, looking wild-eyed at Jory. She was a small, slender, dark-haired woman, her eyes slightly aslant, a mischievous look in them. After a moment she put her arms up out of her wrap and slid them around his neck. "Hello . . . "

He hugged her a little, then moved away.

Gaby Christian, dancer, singer, and longtime television star in a fickle market, was not used to this kind of treatment from the men with whom she chose to share herself. She looked after Jory with an expression of concern. "You mad at me?"

"What for?"

She gestured toward the front of the motel. "Knocking on your door."

"No."

Jory sat down on the couch, picked up his cigarette again: she tossed the wrap aside, came to sit beside him.

"Where were you all day?"

"I was asleep, Gaby. *All day.*" He shook his head, scowling.

She raised her eyebrows, not sure she understood the problem. "Well . . . I enjoyed dinner last night. I thought I'd enjoy it again tonight, if you were with me."

He didn't look up. "What's wrong, Jory?" Gaby said.

Jory closed his eyes, rubbed his head a little: a fretful look. "I never sleep during the day. *Never!* Not that I haven't tried, for most of my life . . ." Then he looked at her, a little suspiciously. "Did you sneak by the desk just now?"

"No, I walked by. The clerk was on the phone." Gaby made a "yak-yak" gesture with one hand.

"She didn't see you?"

"Of course not. Clerks never see witches." She did not say that, after some years of coming to terms with her fame, she had become expert at not being seen when she so desired. It was amazing what a tatty scarf, the wrong color makeup, or the right kind of clothes could do in this regard, and even more amazing what could be achieved by simply setting your face into an expression which no one had ever seen you produce on television. An older actress had advised her never to do soap operas for just this reason: in the course of work, you made too many expressions, and people got to know them all . . . and eventually you had nowhere left to hide when wearing your own face.

Jory got up and began to pace. Gaby's face showed profound regret: an expression few of her television fans had ever seen on her face. "I'm sorry," she said, rather contritely: "you're not in the mood for seductive humor, are you?" Sometimes it was too easy to forget that the coquettish act which had made her famous on TV was not always welcome in people's real lives. But this town made it its business to confuse TV and real life as much as possible . . . .

Jory shook his head. "Anyone can just come right to the door . . . ." he said. He sat down again, this time on the table beside the couch. "Gaby? Do you know what I think? I think something malevolent is going on."

She gave him a dubious look. "Malevolent? I don't like that word."

He got up again and once more started to pace. "When I came back here this morning," Jory said, "after apartment-hunting, I smelled something sweet, deadly sweet. I had a feeling somebody was in the room . . . but before I could look around I had to lie down. Deadly sweet . . . ." He shook his head, rubbed it again. "I slept until . . . just a few minutes ago. And while I was asleep, somebody cleaned up the room."

Gaby slapped her thighs in a "There you have it" gesture. "The maid."

He slapped his thighs right back at her. "No, not the maid. The clerk said she never got to this room today."

"Your brother?"

"I don't think he'd come back and not wake me up . . . ."

Gaby was genuinely mystified now, even a little troubled. Jory stopped, then, and looked at Gaby as contritely as she had looked at him a little earlier. "I'm sorry," he said, and sat down again, reaching out to her to rub her neck affectionately.

"Why?"

"Last night you said I was the first guy in years who hadn't poured his neuroses all over you . . . and here I am, pouring my neuroses all over you."

Last night he had been a breath of fresh air. She had rarely seen such a cheery, amusing, captivating young man, full of certainty in his own wit, desirability and irresistibility. And so, when the evening had begun to, well, to prolong itself, she had made no attempt to stop it. Nor had Jory mentioned her work, her fame or her (putative) fortune once during the whole proceeding, which made him utterly memorable.

Now, though, everything seemed changed. He was very worried about whatever had happened to him, and more worried about his brother . . . and in a town where too many people's lives seemed to include a profound desire to get rid of their relatives, those inconvenient reminders of life before success or stardom, someone who seemed actively interested in being his brother's keeper was likely to stand out.

So Gaby shook her head at him, and clasped his hand. "Nothing neurotic about smelling something deadly sweet in the air. That's just plain spooky." And Gaby looked at him closely. "Though . . . you aren't *really* neurotic . . . are you?"

Jory put the cigarette out, then leaned back on the couch, not looking at her. "The summer I was eight," he said slowly, "I looked out our beach-house window, during a storm, and watched our boat get smashed against the rocks. My father was in it. And so was my mother."

Gaby watched him, very still. "Stu was away at school," Jory said. "When he came for the funeral, he asked me how come I hadn't gone sailing with mom and dad. I told him the truth—I had done something wrong, and Dad was punishing me." He shook his head. "But for some reason, I've always felt that Stu meant I should have been in that boat with them."

Gaby looked at him with concern. "I stay with Stu

as much as I can," Jory said. "I dropped out of school to come out here with him. The only time I don't worry about what he meant is when I'm with him and can see him looking at me with his nice smile . . ."

~~~~~~~~~~

The cold white lab light shone on the features of Stuart Peters, frozen in what definitely was not a nice smile. The expression missed being the classic *risus sardonicus* only in that there was too much fear in the look—eyes squeezed shut so as not to see something, hands frozen as they clawed at a door that would not open, mouth frozen in a scream. Dr. Block and an assistant stood above the stretcher on which Peters was laid out, and Block shook his head a little. Off to one side, Professor Linden stood, looking away.

"It took a long time," Block said calmly, checking the body to make sure that the rigor was not too far advanced. "Some people are a long time dying . . ."

Block checked the flexibility of the joints one last time, then gestured for his assistant to take the body away. After that, he turned to Stephanie Linden. "Stephanie?"

She blinked, holding her lab coat closed around her, and would not look at him. "I'm all right."

"Did he seem interested in our problem?"

The question exasperated her. How could any intelligent scientist *not* be interested by such a problem? She looked at him, then, with the usual annoyance at having to explain the obvious to the blind. "Yes."

"You must get over this repugnance you feel for death, Stephanie," Block said in his "kindly" voice, as if trying to be reasonable to an unreasonable person. "For you to hate death is as foolish as for a live person to hate life."

"I know." She knew no such thing, but there was no other way to get him to be quiet. Stephanie turned away once more, her body rigid—though not with fear. Seeing another lying rigid, so, reminded her too strongly—

—of lying rigid herself: feeling her own body starting to go cold around her; the awful silence of lack of heartbeat, the sound which had shared your life with you for all the years of consciousness—now gone. The fear had stopped that pulse, and the fear, against all hard evidence, continued, even after there was no heart to drive the blood, no blood moving to carry oxygen to the brain, no properly working brain to harbor consciousness—*Well,* she remembered thinking—and *how?*—at the time, *there's one issue settled, at least. Things do go on for a little while, circulation or no circulation. Now let's see if there's a tunnel of light—*

But there was no such thing. The smell and sight of lightning still lingered in her, somehow. *Residual charge? Overload of bioelectricity? 'Persistence' of charge?* She was no expert in the biological sciences. She tried to keep up with the papers, but there was no keeping up with them these days, not if you spent all day reading—and especially not as regarded consciousness issues, where papers multiplied like rabbits on amphetamines.

No matter. It was something to do with the creature. No tunnel of light for Stephanie, no heavenly choirs, no waiting relatives or beings of light. Just darkness, shot through with lightning, and even the lightning beginning at last to fade, so that finally she lay in the darkness, blind, deaf, dumb, stifled, trying to breathe but unable to, trying to move but unable to feel anything but a body stiffening around her: worse than being buried alive, far worse . . . to be buried, live, in your body, *dead,* with no way to escape . . .

Silently, she screamed: for how long, she had no idea. When the jolt came to start her heart again, she was screaming still; through the worst pain of the postoperative stage, while the incision for the augmented pacemaker's electrodes started to heal, she screamed constantly—though through a throat that refused to provide more volume than a whisper, as if already raw from her screams while trapped in the dark. Recovering—if that was the word—she screamed, not from being dead, but from having *been* dead. And from the knowledge that now, the thing that should never happen to a human being more than once, could happen *again* . . .

"You should be grateful to me, Stephanie," Dr. Block said, reaching out to her. "Because of me, you've faced the most terrifying experience of all . . . and gotten it over with."

Over with, she thought with utter horror and scorn. *He knows nothing about it.* Nothing at all. But she said nothing. Block took her shoulders in a fatherly way: and, still fatherly, he pulled apart the lapels of the lab coat to reveal the blinking augmented pacemaker inside. "And now you must rise above bitterness and try to enjoy the life I gave you."

"You?" Stephanie said with intense scorn.

"I," said Block, with no concern at all, no awareness of the irony. "With the help of science, of course."

Arguing with him was futile. He learned nothing from argument—not even scientific argument. That had been one of Stephanie's earliest problems with him—and besides, he now had ways to punish dissension. She had no desire to find herself in that particular dark again—and he would do it, if pushed too far. He had done it to others.

Stephanie grabbed the coat, wrapped it around her again. Mercifully, the phone rang, and she headed for it with intense relief. "Professor Linden here."

After a moment, silently, she held it out to Block. He took it from her.

~~~~~~~~~~~~

Down by the main gate, Jory and Gaby stood in the gateway while the guard spoke into the phone. "Dr. Block? Sorry to disturb you, but there's a young fella here insisting his brother works here, a Professor Stuart Peters, and I can't find his name anywheres in my directory."

There was a pause. "Oh, I see. Sure thing. Thanks."

The guard hung up the phone, went back over to Jory and Gaby. "He just started today, was the reason he wasn't in my directory," said the guard.

"Can I see him?" Jory said.

The guard shook his head. "He's not here."

"What?"

The guard shrugged. "He went out with a field crew to check out the generators north of the Valley."

"When will he be back?"

"Dr. Block said about a week, maybe more."

Jory looked at Gaby, unbelieving: then back at the guard again. "Can I talk to Dr. Block?"

The guard laughed a little, uneasily. "You know what you ought to do, son?" said the guard. "You ought to get you and that lady back into that car and scoot on down to LA, and go dancing." The guard nodded enthusiastically. "She's got nice legs. Girls with nice legs oughta show them off on some public dance floor."

Gaby, for her own part, had heard this often enough before, and she plainly knew when she, and Jory, were being patronized. "Come on, Jory."

Jory's annoyance began to boil over. He stepped quickly toward the guard.

The guard backed hurriedly away, one arm suddenly flung up as if to protect his chest: the amiable look on his face went shocked, afraid. "Didn't mean anything improper, son—"

Jory stepped closer. The guard's hand dropped to his gun. They were practically nose to nose now. To Jory's surprise, the guard hissed, "Get out, son! Get outa here!" It wasn't a threat: it was a plea.

"I want to talk to Dr. Block," Jory growled, grabbing the guard by the coat, pulling him close. The guard staggered back, and his coat pulled out of Jory's grasp: under it was something strange—a black metal box, belted under the guard's breastbone, a mechanical thing with dials and lights. Jory stared at it: the guard clutched it, as if afraid he might lose it.

The guard shook himself, pushed back out of Jory's grasp—again, not with any look of threat, but a terrible and (to Jory) embarrassing show of fear. "Now you know why a big man won't take on a little boy," the guard said. He almost looked over his shoulder as he said it, as if certain someone was watching him. "But don't push too hard; I hate having to depend on this." His hand dropped toward the gun—but didn't touch it.

Slowly Jory let go. The guard backed further away. Jory stepped back, then, and made his way back to Gaby. She looked at him, at the guard, then she took his arm, and they both headed back to the car.

In the guard's box, the phone rang. The guard went quickly to answer it. "Main gate."

The sound of the car's engine was fading down the road back down to the Valley. "—Yes. He went away. —No, sir. No trouble at all. Told him what you said, and he just left. Good night, Dr. Block."

The guard hung up the phone as the night fell silent. He listened a little, then, for anything else— any rising of the wind, any noise as of distant thunder, getting closer. Nothing. Word had gotten around, lately, about sounds like that and what they meant. You didn't want to hear them: you would sooner have young men grabbing you and roughing you up, than . . . *that*.

The guard checked the pacemaker one last time, and went back to the metal chair in his guard's box, hoping desperately that nothing else exciting would happen tonight.

~~~~~~~~~~~~~~~~

A week later, bright morning light fell on the motel, in through the dusty venetian blinds of Jory's room, as Stuart Peters walked in—slowly, carefully, like a convalescent afraid that any sudden move on his part might break something. From the bathroom came the sound of running water. He did not go near the bathroom door, but stood quietly for a few moments looking at himself in the mirror near the hotel door, like a man who sees a stranger.

Jory turned away from the tub he was running to stand up straight in the bathroom doorway, and saw his brother. His face went long with shock. "I didn't hear you come in."

"How are you, Jory?" Stuart said.

The two looked at each other, Jory with more suspicion than anything else. Stuart gazed back at him with a blunted, tired look.

"You don't look glad to see me."

"I've been worried!"

Stuart started to turn away: Jory came to him, reached out and took him by the arms, and stopped him.

"Taking care of yourself?" Stuart said, and again turned away slightly. His face was lined: the nice smile was definitely missing. He looked twenty years older. He glanced around the room, again as if a stranger to the place.

Jory was bewildered. "I kept thinking you'd call, Stu. Almost a whole week. I thought you'd call . . ."

"I was involved in a . . . an experiment at the lab." He would not meet Jory's eyes, and Jory couldn't help but notice it. " . . . You wouldn't understand. I slept and ate in the lab, and . . ."

"Didn't you think I'd be worried?"

"I told someone to call you. Didn't anyone call?" Stuart stepped away, looking out the window into the cheap, bright sunlight.

To Jory, it sounded like a fib, a particularly transparent one. That hurt: he could not remember when his brother had last lied to him. "No," Jory said, following a couple of steps behind his brother. "No messages. I thought you went up north or something."

Once again, his brother wouldn't meet his eyes. "Your tub's going to run over," Stuart said.

Jory gave Stuart an odd look, and headed back for the bathroom. There he adjusted one of the taps, slowing down the running water: but the gesture was purely mechanical. He could hardly concentrate on the bathtub while his brother stood there acting so strangely, almost like some kind of alien being. And moving like he was sick or something— "What kind of experiment?" Jory said.

"The creation of energy. According to law," his brother said, still with his back to Jory as he stood in the bathroom door, "it cannot be created or destroyed, only changed in form. We're trying to break that law. We need more energy than we can legally or scientifically get our hands on. And we'll be needing more and more as time goes on."

Now, finally, he turned, walked back toward his brother, looked at him: but the look was remote and cool. "I warned you, you wouldn't understand."

Now it was Jory's turn to look away, trying for the moment to cover his own bewilderment. The eyes that looked at him now, out of his brother's face, somehow *were not his brother's*. "This girl, Gaby, she thinks I ought to go back to school."

"So do I, Jory." Stuart fiddled uncomfortably with the front of his coat.

"She's out of her mind about me."

"Naturally." But the usual nice smile, the amused smile, the tolerant look, was not there: just an unfocused expression of worry. Of pain . . .? Stuart turned away again.

Jory came after him once more. "I'm thinking of trying to enroll in the university here."

"No. Go back to Kingston, Jory." Stuart wouldn't look at Jory as he said it.

"Why?"

"It means my job."

Jory shook his head, more confused than ever. "How's that, Stu?"

"One of the conditions: no dependents."

"I'm just your kid brother, Stu. I'm not dependent on you."

"Aren't you?"

Stuart's tone of voice brought Jory up short. "Not so anyone would notice," he said.

"I notice."

"Do you, Stu?"

Stuart's expression was definitely pained, as if he was saying something that he had been thinking for a long time—but also as if he had no real desire to say it at all. "Look, Jory . . . you're way past the point where boys are required to become young men. I don't want you to lean on me any more. Make your own decisions and mistakes for a change."

"Gee, can't we be friends?"

"I'm serious, Jory."

Even though Stuart turned toward Jory, and stepped into the bathroom toward where Jory now stood, it was to escape his brother's direct gaze, and Jory knew it. "Leave today, Jory," he said. "I'm moving to the Center anyway."

That was stranger still. Stuart, the lover of home comforts, of having his own place, who had bitched and moaned through seven years of graduate school about the horrors of living in an institution, with no place that was really *yours?* Who *was* this person?

"I got a girl here, Stu." Jory came up behind Stuart, looked at him again as if trying to reach him. Every time he looked at his brother, Stuart looked away. It was like following a shadow, or a ghost. Jory shivered.

"You have girls in Kingston."

"Not like this one. This one knows I'm independently wealthy and loves me anyway." He chuckled a little, more out of bravado than for any other reason. "It just occurred to me: I *am* independently wealthy. I can live anyplace I please."

"Get out, Jory! Pack up and go!" For the first time Stuart turned to look right at him, and there was anger in his voice: but again, as much fear as anger.

"What *is* it, Stu?"

"I want you to go, that's what it is! That's all it is!"

That wasn't all it was, and Jory knew it. "You're a liar, Stu."

"I'm sorry you think that, but I suppose it's easier than facing the truth."

"You tell me the truth, I'll face it."

"I'm sick of having you hang on to me," Stuart said, again with great certainty, as if it was a thought that had occurred many times . . . but a thought which was now being forced out of him, not entirely of his free will. "I'm sick of telling you it's all right when you wake up out of one of those nightmares, sick of pretending I think you're funny when I know you're just a terrified little boy with a big broken heart! It's time you grew up and acted like a man! Now, get out, Jory!"

At least Stuart had the grace to look ashamed after that outburst. Jory looked at his brother through a very brief but profound silence, and then said, "When was the last time I hit you, Stu?"

"You've never hit me."

"I feel like hitting you now."

Stuart backed away a couple of steps. "Be a real man, Jory, not a pair of fists."

Stuart was fumbling uncomfortably with his coat-front again. Something about the way he did it, and about the way he stepped back, suddenly reminded Jory of the way the guard at the gate at Norco had pulled back from him, of the way one arm had come up to shelter the strange something just under his breastbone. Jory reached out to take hold of his brother's arm, which was now in the same protective, or furtive, position. But his brother pushed Jory's hand away.

Stuart held the coat shut. Jory grabbed it, pulled it open, saw what he had seen on the guard: the box with two dials and a couple of blinking lights strapped under his brother's breastbone. "What's that thing?!"

Stuart pushed his hands away again, and as Jory tried to get into the coat for the third time, Stuart lost his balance, wavered, staggered, and fell back into the tub. There was a huge flare of light, and some smoke and steam.

Stuart cried, struggled: his head slipped back under the water. Bubbles rose from his nose as the water from the faucet splashed down onto the water covering his face. Hurriedly Jory reached down into the water, pulled his brother out: held him, shook him—but there was no breath there, no life. Suddenly gone, as if it had been gone for a long time . . .

"Stu? Stu!!"

He held his brother, and wept.

~~~~~~~~~~~~~~~

Motel rooms never look terribly real at the best of times. This one, now filled with harsh daylight and policemen, looked more real than usual.

Jory was having trouble taking it all in. His brother was laid out on a stretcher, being wheeled out by a policeman and a man in a blue coverall with the words COUNTY CORONER on the back. Standing nearby, his back to him, was a big, blocky, solid-looking man in a suit and tie.

Gaby sat beside Jory, watching him. The directness of her glance was hard to bear, after the way his brother had *not* looked at him earlier. "I wasn't going to hit him . . . but he must've thought . . . I was . . . he pulled away . . . and he slipped . . . and . . ." He shook his head. "He exploded, Gaby. Something exploded . . . and I pulled him out of the water . . . right away, Gaby! . . . But he was dead. He was dead just like that . . ."

Behind them, the sound of the stretcher's wheels faded away. The big stocky man came to sit down on the chair nearest the sofa. "I'm Detective-Sergeant Thomas Siroleo, Mr. Peters," he said.

Jory nodded, finding it hard to react, hard to feel

it was important. *Stu . . . Were you even alive? It was like being visited by a zombie. By someone who's stolen my brother's body, or his soul . . . or parts of it. But not my brother. Not really . . . not really . . .*

"You didn't push him, did you?"

Jory turned, scowling fiercely. "Push him?" he said scornfully. "No. I didn't push him."

"The water in the tub was for you?"

Jory nodded. "I was going to take a bath. I don't sleep very well, and some doctor told me if I take a lukewarm bath before I go to bed it might . . . " He broke off, having no desire to talk about his insomnia when such terrible things were going on around him. "What happened to Stu?"

"The coroner thinks the mechanism was defective."

Behind Siroleo, another man in a suit was now standing: a taller man, with white hair. "The water shouldn't have caused a short circuit."

"Mechanism? The thing strapped on his chest?" Jory was still bewildered by that.

"A cardiac pacemaker, but a very unusual one."

"Didn't you know he wore one?" said the coroner.

"No. I don't even know what it is!"

The coroner looked slightly surprised. "It's basically a long-term battery in a control unit . . . it sends rhythmic electric shocks to the heart muscle, and maintains a beat that means normal life for people who otherwise would be dead. But this one has some . . . additions . . . ."

Jory shook his head. "Why would he need that? His heart was okay! He *never* had any heart trouble . . . "

"Hasn't he been in the hospital recently?"

"No!"

The coroner gave him an odd look. "An operation has to be performed. The attachment is inserted directly into the chest cavity. I'll know more after the autopsy,"—this he said as much to Siroleo as to Jory—"but I'd say he's been operated on within the last month."

Jory stood up, looking exasperated. "No! Impossible. I've been with him every day . . ." Then Jory paused, frowned: he turned away from the window, beginning to pace. "Except for a week. When we came out here . . . a week ago . . . he didn't come home, back to the motel I mean . . . for a week . . ."

Siroleo got up too. "Where was he?"

"I don't know." Jory made a helpless gesture. "I called the Center, and they said he'd gone up north or some place . . . a field trip . . . but he said he'd ate and slept in the lab . . . I don't know."

The strangeness of it all, of the brother who had not acted like his brother, kept coming back to him. Part of him wanted to cling to it: *it wasn't your brother, he's not dead,* that part kept whispering. But he knew that part was a liar. Jory rubbed his face, as much to keep from crying as anything else. "I keep thinking, in a minute I'll scream, and wake up . . ."

Gaby looked sorrowfully at Siroleo. "Can't you talk to him later?"

Siroleo didn't look at her. "Where was he? I mean, the Center, what is it?"

"Norco."

Siroleo looked surprised. "The Energy Research Commission?"

Jory shrugged. "Norco."

Siroleo paced for a moment, himself: then he turned back to Jory. "I'd like to talk to you later, Mr. Peters."

Jory got up, headed for the open door, shaking his head. All this simply seemed to be happening too fast. And now someone was missing.... "Where did they take Stu?"

"Jory—" Gaby said.

"No. *I hate this!*" he shouted. "Somebody dies, somebody you thought was going to be there forever, and they come and take him out of the room and you never knew exactly where they took him! Why don't I go with him? Where's he going that I can't go with him?"

Siroleo's sad expression suggested that there was a quick answer to that question, the question itself being very old: but he didn't speak the answer aloud. "His body will be at the County Hospital," Siroleo said. "An autopsy will be performed, and then you can have any mortuary in the city call for the body."

"Please...!" Gaby said.

Siroleo turned to her, not without compassion, and shook his head. "I've always found it best, Miss. Nobody appreciates reality like somebody who's going to have to face it."

He looked back at Jory. "In the morning, Mr.

Peters. We'll help with the disposition of your brother's body, if you want. Then I'd like to see you in my office. About ten. All right?"

"All right. Where's your office?"

"Police headquarters."

"Police headquarters?"

Professor Linden was sitting at her desk, looking up at Dr. Block, and at the stocky man standing beside him.

Block chuckled a little. "Do all beautiful women react guiltily when they hear you're from police headquarters?"

Siroleo laughed, just a breath. "Only the innocent."

Linden gave him a cool and slightly appreciative look, one which left Siroleo briefly wondering exactly what the relationship was between Block and Linden: if he was any judge of such things, there was some kind of power struggle going on. But that was not what he was here to investigate. "He wants to ask you about Professor Stuart Peters," Dr. Block said to Linden.

"I'd heard he was killed," Linden said.

"An accident," said Siroleo. "Would you excuse us?"

Block left. Siroleo glanced after him, waiting until the door was shut, then turned his attention back to Linden.

"Peters," he said, "worked here with you. Was he your assistant, or were you his?"

Linden shook her head. "We worked together, as equals. He was past being anyone's assistant."

It Crawled out of the Woodwork

"Was he operated on here?"

Stephanie Linden took a deep breath. ". . . Yes. Dr. Block performed surgery."

Siroleo perched on the desk: Stephanie looked at him quizzically. "For a minute there . . . I thought you were going to lie to me, Miss Linden."

"*Professor* Linden. —Why should I have lied?" She glanced away.

"Suppose it wasn't a heart attack?" Siroleo said. "Suppose it was some kind of . . . industrial accident? Some firms like to avoid involvement in that sort of thing . . . insurance, bad public relations . . . you know."

She nodded. "But it was a heart attack."

"Yes." He gave her a level look, waiting for more.

Stephanie regarded Siroleo with what he thought was meant to look like slight interest. "You say it as if you don't believe it."

Siroleo shrugged. "The coroner's report was funny, Professor."

She tilted her head to one side, looking away from Siroleo as if bored with an old joke. "If a coroner's report can ever be said to be 'funny'."

"Stuart Peters," Siroleo said, getting up again and starting to pace, "had scar tissue as fresh as tomorrow morning's milk. So the operation had to have taken place after he came here."

"And no one said it didn't," said Stephanie, folding her hands.

"But he had to undergo a complete physical before he left Kingston, New York. Your own company insisted. Now, I've seen those records, Professor. If he'd been in any better health, they'd have given him a morning exercise show on TV." He paused in his strolling back and forth, looked at Stephanie. "A heart attack just wasn't in the cards for Stuart Peters."

She looked up at him challengingly. "What do you deduce from all this, Mr. Siroleo?"

"Shock or fright," Siroleo said, "properly induced, can cause a heart attack."

"He was working right beside me when the attack happened." Linden studied her hands. "Do you think I could shock or frighten anyone . . . to the point of death?"

Siroleo didn't answer for a moment. Rhetorical questions like that, in his experience, were rarely rhetorical. They usually just barely concealed someone's attempt to hide the truth from you—or to reveal it without seeming to. "What kind of work?" he said at last.

Linden's head was bowed. She looked up, glanced around at the equipment, the computers, all the paraphernalia. It looked intimidating, and Siroleo knew she meant for him to be intimidated. "Would you understand?"

"Probably not," Siroleo said, declining the intimidation. He had not signed up to be a physicist, and therefore felt no obligation to feel substandard because he didn't understand what physicists did. He strolled away a little distance, among the blinking machines. "Could I just look around on my own?"

"No." He looked at her sharply. Stephanie got up, went to him. "You must be accompanied by . . ."

"I'm not a bad security risk."

She made an I-can't-help-it gesture. "I personally do not create or enforce security regulations at Norco. I merely obey them. You'll need higher permission than mine."

"Dr. Block's?"

"He's Director in Chief."

"I guess I'd better talk to him, then." Siroleo stepped away.

"If you like. Mr. Siroleo?"

He turned and smiled at her, amiably enough. "*Sergeant* Siroleo. We all like our titles, Professor."

She nodded. "Dr. Block isn't in his office now," Stephanie said. "You'll find him in the Pit."

"The Pit?"

She nodded toward the heavily shielded door. "The energy chamber. We call it the Pit."

She went over to the switches which controlled the door, and pressed one. The door slid open. Siroleo looked at it thoughtfully. He was surprised, though, to see Linden slam her fist against the heavy wall, leaning her head against the wall by the switch-panel. Once, and twice, she hit the wall, hard.

Bemused, he stepped over to her. "Are you all right?"

She tossed her head back, like someone trying to get her breath. "Yes. Of course. Go on, Sergeant."

"But you look upset. What's the matter?"

She was gasping for breath now. He took her by the upper arms, turned her around to face him. "What is it?"

Linden couldn't look at him. Her face turned away, she said desperately, "I can't! I just can't!"

She broke away from him with such violence that the motion hurt Siroleo's hands, and ran out the laboratory door.

~~~~~~~~~~

In the motel, Jory sat at the bare little desk, under the unforgiving glare of the desk lamp, and stared at an inane ceramic bunny rabbit which was someone's idea of what to leave on motel desks these days. "What was that detective's name?" he said dully.

From where she sat on the couch, Gaby looked over at him from a backlit cloud of cigarette smoke. "Siroleo."

"Is that a Greek name?"

"I don't know."

"He said around ten?" Jory said.

She nodded. "In the morning."

He fiddled with things on the desk, leaned back, ran his hands through his hair, moaned softly. "But first there's a night to get through . . ."

Gaby got up and strolled over to him slowly. "We can go for a drive."

"Get away from me, Gaby." He didn't say it particularly rudely, more as an acknowledgment that she was sexy, and having her too close made it hard for him to think—especially now, when his body cried out for relief from the things it was being forced to think about.

Gaby, not insulted, turned away and sat down on the couch again. Jory's unease was contagious, and she felt around for something harmless to say, something distracting. "What was his name," she said suddenly, "the friend who suggested you call me when you got into town?"

"I don't remember," Jory said. "I made it up."

She blinked at that, then became slightly suspicious. "Did you really see all my TV shows?"

"I think so."

"What made you call me?"

"Your legs. You have very fine legs . . . ." He didn't look at her when he spoke of her legs, but then Jory turned to her and said, " . . . Someone at Norco killed my brother, Gaby."

The sudden directness, the concentration in those eyes, scared her a little. Jory got up. "Can I borrow your car?"

"I'll drive."

"No. You stay here, Gaby." He got up, went to get his coat. There was none of his usual impulsiveness about it, though—it was more as if he was sleepwalking.

"You're going up there?"

"Yes."

~~~~~~~~~~~~~

In the laboratory, Detective Siroleo stood looking at the long corridor behind the open door. He heard the vague rumbling down at the other end, and was drawn toward it.

Behind him, a woman's hand reached out, touched the switch that shut the door to the lab.

He looked over his shoulder at this, then paused

and looked down again at the door at the other end of the corridor. Its window flickered, and the rumbling got louder, as if something was responding to the sound of the outer door shutting. Slowly Siroleo walked down the corridor, then paused once again, looking over his shoulder toward the lab door.

The rumbling was beginning to get into his head, but Siroleo kept on going, down toward the door at the corridor's end. The thick window of green glass was just on a level with his head. He looked through it.

He saw—what, he couldn't say. At first, his eyes, seeing nothing in there familiar but walls and ceiling and floor, refused to make sense of the room's contents. But after several long seconds, he began to see a shape, a form . . . and more than that. *If you took a thunderstorm and locked it in a room until it was angry, he thought, it would look and sound like this.* The sound of electric power lines fizzing and overloading was in the sound he heard: and wind and thunder, rattling together, and a kind of beast's scream, subdued at the moment, but slowly getting louder—

The thing making the noise was big. Sometimes it looked vaguely man-shaped; then it had arm- and leg-shaped protuberances, and a blunt blob that might have been a head. Then, as if it was too angry or too unfocused to hold such a shape, the thing collapsed back again into a cloud, dark- and light-shot, writhing, roiling, and flickering with power from inside—as if there was lightning held captive inside it, trying to get out.

Siroleo stared through the window, transfixed.

The thing came toward the window, perceiving him: and the howl got louder. Siroleo had seen a lot of odd and ugly things in his time, a great deal of death; a lot of blood and pain. But he had never seen anything that so pullulated with death as *this* thing, with all its flashing and screaming and rage.

He caught his breath, backed hurriedly away from the far door, and ran back down the corridor to the door that gave on the laboratory. He hammered on it, tried to find a way to open it. There was none. He called for help—

But no help came. Only, outside the door, near the switch, her back turned to the window, stood Professor Linden, breathing hard. She swung around, out of his view, and went hurriedly, as if she feared she might change her mind, to the switch: hit one.

The lab door slid open. Siroleo staggered out of it, grabbed her by the shoulders. "What is it?" he yelled at Linden, shaking her. *"What in the world is it?"*

She shook her head, still gasping for air. "Get out! Quick! Go!"

"No," he said, trying to get hold of himself, as much for her sake as his own. "No, it's all right—"

"It's not all right! Get out of here! He'll kill you!"

"He won't," Siroleo said, trying desperately to calm her enough to get some explanations. "He won't kill anyone—"

"He'll kill me!" Stephanie Linden cried between gasps, shaking her head in frantic denial. "For doing this . . . He'll kill me—again!"

Again?? Siroleo thought, and looked at her, stunned.

She felt about for the buttons of her lab coat, pulled the coat open, showed him the pacemaker. "Just get out," she said. "Quick. Don't worry about me. I've already died once!"

Siroleo shook his head, not sure what to make of this—but certain he had to get her out of there, as much for reasons of potential evidence as anything else. "No," he said, "come on, I'll take you out of here. Come on—"

She pushed him away. "No! Just go! Go! Go!"

From behind them came the slow, rather jolly European voice. "Go *where*, Stephanie?"

With horror, she looked up: then her head bowed in hopelessness. Siroleo's teeth set: Linden's look was the look of a slave, almost escaped, now recaptured on the brink of freedom.

~~~~~~~~~~~~~~~

The lamps were on down at the Norco main gate. It was quiet: the wind breathed only softly in the trees. The guard who sat by the gate was bored, and pleased to be so.

Just out of earshot, a ways down the rutted road, in the darkness, a car pulled softly to the side and shut its engine down. A woman and man sat in the car together, the woman smoking nervously; while the man sat, holding some silent argument with himself, frozen in indecision . . .

"You've seen it then," Dr. Block said to Siroleo.

Siroleo, standing by Stephanie Linden, looked at the gun in Block's hand, and decided not to do anything sudden. It was a Glock, and looked very well-kept: and like most other guns of its kind, it had no safety. "What is it?" he said. "Where did it come from?"

"It's pure energy, Sergeant," said Block. "Pure, unadulterated, unminimized power." He moved slowly toward them. "In the words of the cleaning woman who unwittingly gave it life, 'It crawled out of the woodwork.'"

"You haven't tried to destroy it?" Siroleo said.

"Why would I want to do that . . . even if I could?"

Block was so completely in control of himself that it frightened Siroleo . . . but he was not about to show it. Block, meanwhile, was being careful not to get close enough to Siroleo for him to do anything sudden about the gun, even if he wanted to. Now the director paused by the door, glanced down through that window while still holding the gun on Siroleo and Linden.

"You aren't afraid of it?"

Block shook his head. "A scientist learns not to be afraid of things he doesn't understand."

Dr. Block perched himself comfortably on one of the nearby desks, wearing the pleased expression of a man with a chance to hold forth on a favorite subject. "A few members of my staff tried to destroy it. But energy cannot be destroyed. So they decided to destroy me." And he glanced with amusement at Linden.

"We didn't want to destroy you," she said, rather angrily. "Only to protect ourselves."

He gave Siroleo a look which translated as "How typical." "Simple heart surgery," he said, "brought them to reason. One by one, I had them terrified to death, and one by one I gave them back their lives—lives they own only so long as I do not cut off the power that makes their hearts beat."

Siroleo looked with shock at Stephanie, suddenly understanding the look of hatred she had given the pacemaker. "You see," Block said, "I have almost total control over that energy force in there . . . It would eagerly suck the power out of that pacemaker, if I allowed it to."

"Is he insane?" Siroleo said softly to Linden. Stephanie began doing up her coat again. "I wish he were," she said bitterly. "The insane are forgivable."

"Not insane, Sergeant. At worst, obsessed. Think of it: a small lifeless thing, like a ball of black dust, huddled against a baseboard in a dustless corner." He gestured expansively. "What is it? Where does it come from? Why does it suddenly live when it is fed common energy?"

Why do I always wind up with the nutsos? Siroleo thought, desperate to find some way out of this situation . . . especially since *this* nutso was more than usually dangerous. "Questions like that are always interesting, Dr. Block," Siroleo said softly. "And they deserve to be answered. But not at the cost of human life."

Block shook his head. "The wonderful questions are always answered at the cost of human life," he said, wagging a finger in an amiable and didactic way. "Remember how we wondered about the atom b—"

Siroleo leapt straight for the hand that had the gun in it, grabbed it two-handed. The two of them struggled for a moment. Block was more the didact, though, than Siroleo: Siroleo might not be a theoretical physicist, but he had had a lot of experience at rough-and-tumble in his time. He forced Block back against the wall near the switches for the doors, hammered the gun out of his hand. It flew to one side.

Professor Linden stooped to pick it up. She straightened and said, calmly, "Stay clear, Sergeant."

Block accessed a huge rush of strength from somewhere, and pushed Siroleo away. Just as the police officer was reaching out a hand to say "Don't!" to Professor Linden, she fired.

Block slid down the wall, to lie there slumped and bleeding.

~~~~~~~~~~

Outside, in the car, the man and the woman faced each other in the darkness.

"Do you want to go back, Gaby?"

"Do you?"

He paused, stared through the windshield toward the faint lights ahead of them, the gate-lights of Norco, visible through the brush. "I don't know. I want to go up to that guard and make him let me in, knock him out if I have to, but I can't decide if that's what I really ought to do. —I can't make decisions, Gaby."

"I'll wait here," Gaby said. "Go ahead."

"Don't help me!" Jory snapped.

She blinked. "I'm sorry, Jory. Have a cigarette?"

And she waited.

There was a long pause. Then Jory got out of the car, and slowly headed off into the dark: paused, and strode up toward the gate.

In the lab, Professor Linden sat at a console, her face in her hands, sobbing. Siroleo touched her arm gently, trying to console her, but there seemed little he could say.

"I didn't want . . . to do that," she said between sobs. "It isn't right . . . to kill someone . . . just because . . . you can't forgive him . . ."

Siroleo waited. She recovered herself a little, enough to take Siroleo by the arm for a moment and look up at him earnestly through the tears.

"When it first appeared," she said, " . . . he looked at it as a scientist would look. Curious . . . even frightened. He was sure, we were all sure, it could be controlled and studied. But we knew that if our control slipped, even for a second, it would kill when it was loose." She shook her head, at the memory of who knew what horror.

By the time we're finished cleaning this up, Siroleo

thought, *there's going to be a lot more than just one murder to investigate . . . How many 'missing-persons' cases will turn out to end up on the doorstep of that thing in there? . . .*

"It would kill, mindlessly, indiscriminately," Professor Linden said. "So we tried to destroy it . . . but he didn't want it destroyed." Her face went dark with rage. "It was his discovery, he said. It was *his*, and he would solve the mystery of it. *He* would . . ."

And with great clarity, from the other side of the room, a voice suddenly said, "Every man wants to solve one mystery . . . before he dies."

Block had managed to drag himself back to his feet. Bracing himself against the wall near the door, he was groping for the panel with the buttons set in it: he hit the second one, the one which opened the door at the far end of the corridor.

From down that hallway came the sound of the thunderstorm pent up in that room, now about to get out and make someone very sorry for its confinement. Siroleo headed toward Block, but Linden turned and ran immediately for the main door to the laboratory, yanked at it, hammered on it.

"He locked it!" she cried. "He's locked it!"

Siroleo turned to see the writhing, blinding cloud-shape come gliding down the hall. He backed away from the open doorway in horror as the wind of the thing's coming grew stronger, and papers began to fly about in the lab. Block slumped down beside the door, in the monster's path.

Siroleo and Linden ran back together, looking for

a hiding place—if there was really anywhere one could hide from that thing. All they could manage, finally, was to crouch behind a desk, huddled down and shivering like children trying to escape some punishment which at heart they know to be inescapable. The cloud-thing came out into the lab, hovered briefly about Block's slumped form. Sparks shot about as it enveloped him, and moved away.

The creature paused briefly to stretch a filament of smoke toward a lightbulb hanging from the ceiling: the bulb blew out, the fixture from which it hung sparked, shorted, melted. The creature kept going, drifting onward into the equipment in its path; it passed right through a table, melting some things, vaporizing or vanishing others, destroying everything on it. It drifted close to the desk, paused . . .

Then it headed for the lab door. Roaring, showing no sign of passing a barrier, it plunged on through, shattering or devouring everything it touched: free at last, free to hunt as it desired . . . .

~~~~~~~~~~~~~~

Outside in the dark, Jory made his way through the brush between the rutted road and the gate. He paused for a moment in the darkness, hearing a strange noise coming from the direction of the Norco main buildings: a howling of wind, a crack and fizz of lightning, of electricity run amok. For the moment, he stood irresolute, wincing, as an old memory teased at the back of his brain—

~~~~~~~~~~

Inside, the creature tore down the hallway, seeking for more to devour. A staff member wearing a pacemaker came out of a doorway, backed away screaming "No! No!"—not that it mattered. A moment later his pacemaker was sucked dry of power, sparked and dead. He himself was gone, everything in him, probably down to the shells of the atoms that made him up, sucked dry or converted to energy—nothing left to blow away. The creature plunged on, looking for more . . . .

~~~~~~~~~~

In the lab, Siroleo was on the phone, having somehow managed to get an outside line despite the chaos. Having dealt in rapid succession with his precinct commander and the chief of police, he was now shouting at someone high up in the local Civil Defense organization. "No, I don't know what to suggest," he shouted over the howling, not too close at the moment, but not nearly far enough away for his comfort.

The voice, seeming miles away, squawked in his ear. "Tanks?" Siroleo repeated aloud, rolling his eyes slightly. Tanks were likely to be about as impervious as tissue paper to this thing.

Behind him, Linden said hurriedly, "No! No tanks, or guns! They'll work for it, not for us. It'll consume *any* form of energy. Kinetic, chemical, it's not fussy . . ."

"What?" he shouted at the phone. "No. So long as we stay in the dark, we're as safe as we can be." He listened again to one more inane suggestion, something about atomics. *Just what the Valley needs* . . . "—No. She said *there's no way to destroy it*. What part of 'no way' was it you didn't understand?!"

"We have to *control* it," Linden said, but she sounded desperate.

"How?" Siroleo asked.

"Get it back into the Pit!"

Siroleo thought grimly of the old story about belling the cat. "*How?*"

"The Pit has its own generators. If we can cut off the power everywhere else . . ."

It was better than nothing. "Cut off all the power in this area!" Siroleo shouted down the phone. "Quick! I'll kill as much of it as I can from here."

He got Linden up, and together they started to move from piece to piece of machinery in the lab, shutting everything down, hoping against hope that there would be enough time. The roaring, the howling was getting closer again . . .

~~~∿∿∿∿∿∿~~~

There are spots on the earth that astronauts see, not as patches of vague glitter, but as little holes of light, as if they were looking through a window into a lighted room. The strip between Brussels and Amsterdam is one: the astronauts call it "the Belgian Window." Metropolitan Tokyo is another: so is the corridor between New York and Washington. And maybe the brightest of the windows is the Los Angeles area.

The astronauts would have been very surprised, had any of them looked down at that spot at this moment, to see the upper "pane" of the Los Angeles Window just go out, go black: the whole irregular oblong of the San Fernando Valley simply turned off, like a light switched off in a room . . .

At the front gate of Norco, the guard sat, bored . . . when suddenly, the lights around him all went out: the sparkle of Valley lights below, and the lights at the gate.

Behind him, the wind began to rise. He heard the roaring, looked over his shoulder through the gates, and slowly stood up. He was having trouble catching his breath. He pulled open his jacket, looked at the pacemaker, and saw what he had been warned might happen if he broke the rules—saw the lights of the pacemaker dim, the battery failing. Behind him, the howling grew louder.

As the guard fell to the pavement and writhed there, Jory ran up toward him through the darkness, and found him lying on the ground. He saw the pacemaker, the last glimmer of its lights winking out. Jory stared through the gates, heard the wind, heard the thunder, and knew that he was close to what had killed his brother. The wind and the thunder reminded him of something else, too—that day by the lake, the boat running into the rocks, smashing as the thunder shouted above it . . .

Not again. Oh, not again . . .

He stood there struggling with his fear and with the sound, suddenly clear through the tumult, of his mother's scream, of his father's shout—more surprise than anything else—as the boat hit the rocky escarpment that jutted out into the lake so close to the old summer house. How long, now, had he been trying to avoid hearing those sounds? . . . even to the extent of not being able to sleep, for fear of hearing them in his dreams. Now, though, alone out here in the dark night and the cold wind, Jory found that even wakefulness was no defense. His nightmares had come hunting him. Here, if he was ready for it, was a chance to hunt them back . . .

It was past time for equivocations. His mind was finally made up. Jory ran through the dark gates, into the darkness and toward the storm.

~~~~~~~~~~~~~~~

In the corridors of Norco, the flickering cloud went roiling about, hungry, looking for power, and not finding any. Its roaring got louder. It was furious. There had been plenty to eat, before: electricity, at least, tastier and less work than eating mere dead matter. Power was best, predigested, the only thing that really quenched its thirst: the thirst it had never not known, the thirst which made it madder moment by moment. Behind it, though, in the bad place, the place where it had not been free . . . back there it could feel plenty of power. All it could drink. And other things too . . .

It churned and roiled in indecision. It had been kept so long in the same place, against its will: first being fed only dribs and drabs of the fire which made it feel fit and whole, then gradually fed more and more . . . but still pent up, kept away from an *elsewhere* where there was more and more of what it wanted, endless amounts of it.

Now it was out in that 'elsewhere', but it had found little worth the visit: brief spurts of energy sucked from tiny compact storage sources, and the more difficult and tasteless energy trapped in matter. Beyond that lay what seemed only a great empty darkness, devoid of food.

But, still, it was *outside* now, free . . . .

It roared in pain at the choice. It wanted both options. It could not have them.

Slowly, it turned, and made its way, shrieking, back toward the lab.

~~~~~~~~~~~~~~

In the laboratory, Siroleo bent anxiously over Linden, who was collapsed over the desk behind which they had hidden, gasping as if for her last breath. Siroleo couldn't understand the problem: unless it was good old-fashioned shock, which he wished he had the leisure to succumb to.

"What is it?" he said, shaking her slightly. "What's the matter?"

She shook her head, unable to speak for a moment, and then found strength or breath to gasp,

"It's taking . . . the power . . ."

~~~~~~~~~~~~~~~

Down the hallway where the thing had just passed, Jory ran, smelling ozone—on the track of the storm, following the trail of it. He came to a T-junction, looked up and down it—then heard the sound, and saw, for the first time, the roiling cloud—

He ran at the thing, not knowing what it was, not caring. As he got close, his skin prickled with the sheer threat of it. Shouting with uncontrolled anger, and with a bizarre near-elation, he ran at it. *I dare, at last, I dare . . .!* And to his astonishment, almost to his fury—it went *away*, hurrying from him, pursuing something else.

Swearing, Jory ran after it.

~~~~~~~~~~~~~~~

In the laboratory, Professor Linden collapsed on the desk. The door blew open, and Siroleo took cover as the creature came storming in: fury wrapped in lightning, looking for a meal, and heading for the only one it could find . . . the scent and taste of concentrated, free-flowing power, down in the Pit.

It made its shrieking way through the now-dead lab equipment, papers flying in all directions. Jory came staggering in the door behind it, like vengeance hunting vengeance, unwilling to let it go. The creature ignored him, plunging instead toward the open laboratory door, starting to make its way down the corridor into the Pit.

Jory would have gone straight after it. Siroleo was before him, though. The detective made a staggering dash for the switches in the wall, paused for only a second to watch the horrible thing go roiling down the hallway, and hit the button that controlled the door.

It slid shut with a clang. Siroleo slumped against the wall, gasping.

Jory stood still and looked around the lab, gasping too; afraid, but also, in a way, satisfied, and still strangely elated.

"It's under control," Siroleo gasped, "for the moment." He now found himself gasping as if he had suddenly had one of the pacemakers installed as well. He pulled himself away from the wall against which he had been leaning, and took a few steps into the middle of the lab, where he stood briefly, looking like a man who has just seen his death pass him by within inches, with no power to stop it . . . knowing it was luck that made it happen, and no force at his own command.

Slowly Siroleo walked over to where Linden lay collapsed, to see if she still breathed. She did, if just barely: he leaned her back in her chair to help her breathe more easily. At least the lights on the pacemaker were shining again, and one of them was blinking on and off, on and off, steadily as a heartbeat.

He took Linden's wrist, feeling for the pulse. It was weak, at the moment, but there: and though he was no expert at this, it felt like it was getting stronger all the time.

Siroleo gazed around the wrecked lab, shaking his head a little at all the work, and the explanations, that lay ahead of him. *How many more murders of Block's are we going to have to clean up? he thought. And there's a nice legal problem for you. Is it murder, if you bring the person back to life afterward? Or does this count as 'assault with a deadly weapon'?* . . . He could see where this investigation was likely to go on for a long while.

There might even be a promotion in it for him. Siroleo shook his head at the thought, though. He wasn't sure he wanted a promotion, not at *this* price: the knowledge that, somewhere up in these quiet, sunny hills, was something that would have to be fed, and carefully kept prisoner, forever, or until people figured out how to destroy energy . . . whichever came first.

A long time, either way. And if by some mischance it should get out . . .

That wasn't likely to be his problem, though. At least Siroleo very heartily hoped not . . .

Footsteps behind him made him turn: Jory Peters was standing there, looking around at the destruction. "Are you still going to want to see me in your office?" Jory said.

Siroleo looked at him wearily, and smiled, just a little. "In a slightly different capacity," he said. "Just call the office, tomorrow, and if you're planning a change of residence, leave me a number where I can reach you." He turned away, contemplating the mess and starting to think about who to call first . . . .

~~~~~~~~~~~~

And Jory stood there for a moment more, getting his own breath back, looking around him as the lights came back up. Vengeance was over now . . . not that he had truly had any: but he had found the courage to try. *It'll have to do* . . . Soon enough the loneliness for his brother would come back: Jory knew that very well. Never again to see the nice smile . . . or anything else of Stuart's but a few personal possessions, the furniture from the old house they had shared . . . . It would be hard.

And for a long time, he suspected, when he thought of his brother, he would be able to see nothing but lightning wrapped in cloud, and screaming: the thing that killed Stuart, now imprisoned down at the end of that hall.

There was always the question of punishment . . . . but punishment was for those who could understand it. Even in the brief brushes he had had with the creature, no more than a long look down a hallway, Jory had clearly felt its elemental quality. How did you punish a storm? It was only doing what it had no choice but to do—or perhaps, in this thing's case, what it had been made to do.

At least it was imprisoned. That would have to do . . . not just for the time being, but forever. Meanwhile

. . . he would have to find a way to make life seem worth living. *At least,* he thought, *I'll have a little help.*

Slowly he walked out of the lab, to make his way back down to the car, and Gaby.

~~~~~~~~~~

Much later, when the crime teams were busy overrunning the inside of Norco, Siroleo stood out in the parking lot, looking down on the lights in the Valley, thinking about the Law of Conservation of Energy . . . a principle which states that energy can be changed in form, but that it cannot be either created or destroyed.

It was true of all energy, he guessed . . . including (to judge from the last day or so) the energy of genius, of madness, of the heart, of the atom. And somehow, regardless, it had to be lived with. It had to be controlled, channeled for good, held isolate from evil . . . and somehow, *peaceably,* lived with.

He looked back up at the Norco buildings, from which a low humming sound came: the sound of something being quietly, continually, fed. And he shivered.

Going to be a cold one tonight, Siroleo thought, glancing up at the clear sky, the stars above: and he went back inside, back to work.

~~~~~~~~~~

DIANE DUANE'S first novel, The Door into Fire, *was published in 1979, when she was still in her mid-twenties. Since then she has had published more than twenty science fiction and fantasy novels, including a number of* Star Trek *novels that have become bestsellers. Diane has developed* Star Trek *stories in more media than any other author. In addition to novels, she writes extensively for the screen, including more than forty animation scripts for every major animation studio and the memorable episode "Where No One Has Gone Before" for* Star Trek: The Next Generation.

Diane Duane lives in Ireland with her husband, UK fantasy author Peter Morwood, and two cats. Their two-hundred-year-old cottage in Wicklow is also the improbable home to several overworked computers and any number of intergalactic battles.

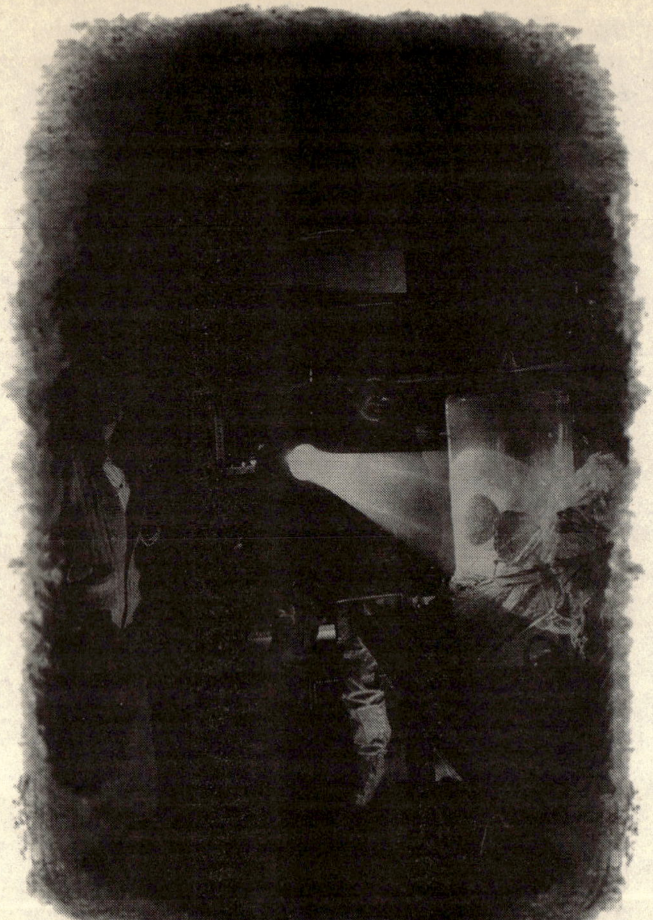

The haunted house story is as old as houses themselves. Shirley Jackson's Hill House stands head and shoulders above the rest, but it's in good company nonetheless. Stephen King has written about the Overlook Hotel, Richard Matheson about hell house, H. P. Lovecraft about a score of eerie New England mansions, Anne Rivers Siddons about the house next door, and hundreds more.

The horror devotee knows what will happen when the haunted house door is open. Boards will creak, mysterious voices will moan, danger will be close at hand. But every haunted house is different, and you will find as you read on that the old Abrams house, as imagined by Manny Coto in his Outer Limits *screenplay, and brought to you here by Howard Hendrix, is not exactly what you think it might be.*

If These Walls Could Talk

Adaptation by Howard V. Hendrix
Original Screenplay by Manny Coto

RAIN FELL through a darkness strobed with lightning and cracked by thunder. Inside the old Abrams place, though, beneath the light of a dozen scattered candles, young lovers kissed deeply, feeling warm and safe in each other's arms—despite the sudden puffs of wind pushing through the disrepair of a house long abandoned, drafts making the candles flicker, filling the house with unidentifiable sounds.

"Did you hear that?" Derek asked, rising abruptly

on his elbows, nearly dislodging Nadia from on top of him. Through wire-rimmed glasses he stared about the room, dazed by Nadia's passion and his own but still hearing it: a voice made of dark wind, moaning, calling.

"Hear what?" Nadia asked, her confusion turning to peevishness. How could Derek be so distracted when here she was right in his face, practically naked, dressed only in panties and open shirt over a loose bra?

"That sound—" he began, disturbed by its persistence.

"You mean like somebody moaning?" Nadia asked, rising back from him, looming above him.

"Yeah," Derek said, pushing himself more upright on the couch.

"That was me," Nadia said nonchalantly, even a bit aggressively, as she shoved him firmly back down onto the couch and resumed her passionate kissing of his shirtless neck and chest. He found her will hard to resist, especially when her kisses and caresses sapped his own will and drove his fears further away with each passing moment.

The calling, reverberant moan came again, though—much louder and more insistent this time. So loud it jolted Derek bolt upright, so fast that he almost knocked Nadia over.

"Derek—!"

"I heard it again," he said, hitching up and buttoning his pants as he got quickly to his feet. Something wasn't right about that sound, a deep distorted undertone that he didn't like at all. It made him feel suddenly cold, like a scream from a nightmare.

"Heard what?"

"A voice. There's someone else here."

Nadia flopped down grumpily into the spot on the couch Derek had just vacated.

"Look," she said. "Maybe we should've just gone to the ridge, like you said first. You wanna just go?"

"No," Derek said firmly, grabbing up one of the many candles placed about the room on the floor and ledge. "No. I'm just going to look around real quick. See if we're alone. I'll be right back."

"Well," Nadia began sharply as she watched him leave their circle of light, "I'm sure as hell alone."

Heavy flickering candle held out before him, Derek, still shirtless, made his way into a foyer as dark and bare and abandoned-looking as the rest of the boarded-up house. The moaning voice or voices sounded without a break now.

"Somebody here?" Derek asked the darkness of a large empty downstairs parlor. "Hello?"

Something—the wind or a wet scuttling sound like a blast of rain—made him shift the candle toward his left, toward a large staircase. The stairway must have been imposing once, but now layers of paint and wallpaper hung peeling from the walls beside it. The boards of the stairs stood cracked and dry. Dust webbed the banister and a number of the balustrade posts supporting it were broken out. Not a very inviting prospect.

Derek started up the stairs toward the second floor, candle held before him. The treads and risers of the staircase squeaked noisily beneath his every step, an annoying sound drowned out only occasionally by peals of thunder from the storm raging outside.

Hearing Derek climbing the stairs, Nadia shook her head in frustration. She needed a good buzz to gentle her down about now, and she was going to give herself one, Derek's anti-drug mommy be damned. Reaching over the arm of the couch, Nadia found the joint she had stashed there amid the clutter on the old crate end table. She took it and lit up, dragging a deep inhalation of pot smoke into her lungs. The creaking stairs and clashing thunder faded from her consciousness as she drifted into reverie. Yes, this felt good—the contemplative yet strong high guaranteed by the sativa/indica crosses of the smoke she most favored.

Glancing about the room, at the temple-of-love candles everywhere and the empty beer and wine bottles, Nadia smirked to herself. Yes, Derek's mother would most certainly disapprove—especially if she'd known it was partly Nadia's idea to come here. Not that they'd had much choice, of course. The weather had seen to it that their original plan—going up to Inspiration Point, on the ridge—was a washout. This was a fine and private second choice, until Derek got spooked.

Nadia looked at the bottles scattered about and almost laughed. Derek's mother had firmly steered him away from drugs and he drank very little anyway. Maybe his mom was a recovering alcoholic or something, she speculated. The bottles here were leftovers from other nights, when locals had used the abandoned

Abrams place as a party zone or transients had made it their flophouse. No alcohol had touched Derek's lips or her own all evening.

Still, she thought, that was part of Derek's appeal for her. He was like that guy in the comics her brother used to read when they were kids. Shy, innocent, sort of nerdy. Bespectacled high school straight-arrow, but take off his shirt and he was Spider-Man, or at least had a nice bod. That was Derek to a tee. He probably thought he was heroically defending her from something, even now.

A cold wind blew past her, and she had the odd sensation that someone or something was watching her, unseen eyes caressing her body. Her bare legs pebbled with gooseflesh. She took another deep drag on the joint as thunder pealed outside.

This time, she heard something. A sound like a strangled groan. Derek's voice, curiously muffled, calling out "Nadia!"

"Derek?" she asked, not loudly enough. No answer. "Dammit."

She put the joint down on the crate end table then grabbed up her holes-in-the-knees jeans from the far end of the couch. She bounced herself into her jeans and grabbed the flashlight that Derek, in his infinite wisdom, had neglected to take when he went off to investigate his mysterious sounds. She clicked on the flashlight and headed toward the stairs. At the base of the stairs she thought she heard another muffled groan and the sound of something shifting—upstairs.

"Derek!" she said, starting up the creaking stairs.

"This is totally immature."

No answer came. She made her way to the hallway on the second floor, playing the light from the flash before her, up and down and side to side, as if to ward off she knew not what.

No Derek. Frustrated and nervous, she shone the light into corners and further down the hall.

"Derek!" she called again, more urgently. No answer. "I'm taking off!"

Still nothing. She moved a few paces further down the hall.

"I'm serious!"

A puff of wind blew past her, followed by a strong, low sound, as if the whole building had suddenly inhaled. Nadia sensed something shifting, moving, in the floor and walls, the wind reaching out toward her, snarling "YOU!"

Nadia cried out and bolted back up the hallway, to the landing of the stairs, and started back down the stairs almost whimpering in fear. She was not even halfway down when the flashlight's beam and a flash of lightning together caught something that halted her in midstep, something so startling she almost lost her balance.

The walls and stairs were shifting, moving, organic and alive, flowing like waves of peristalsis—flowing toward her.

"God, oh God—" she said, feebly trying to backpedal up the stairs.

"YOU!" said the snarling voice, dark and cold as the night wind.

Nadia fell as the fabric of the stairway itself heaved around her ankles and began pulling her inexorably down, into the waiting maw of the devourer. Her flashlight spun away into darkness. She screamed and screamed, her hands bloody from grabbing and breaking away the rotted balustrade posts, her nails torn off where she tried to grip the treads and risers of the stairs—to no avail.

Inexorably she disappeared, like a particle of food engulfed by the membrane of a hungry cell, caught in the trembling tenacious grip of life devouring life, until only her blood on the stairs remained. Then that too was gone, vanished as completely as a summer cloudburst upon the desert.

In a brightly lit townhouse in the city of Vancouver, Levi Mitchell sat typing on an old Valentine at his cluttered desk. His glance flicked past a framed desktop photograph of himself and his late wife Carrie on a canoeing trip, then moved back to the image of Lynda Tillman, the woman being interviewed on the talk show playing on his big screen TV.

"Would you consider yourself an expert in the subject of ghosts or supernatural phenomena?" asked the bespectacled and rather unctuous host.

"Not at all," said Lynda, a dark-haired woman in her mid-to-late thirties who seemed uncomfortable with the interview process yet determined to get through it. "I'm just an average citizen who thinks that there's more out there than what we experience through our five senses. I think people need to be made aware of that."

Mitchell repeated the words sotto voce as he typed them up for his transcript of the show. Tillman's "Jane Doe" approach was a wise one, he thought. Get the audience sympathizing....

"But you must admit," the host countered, "that it's a lot harder for people to believe in ghosts nowadays. After all, it is the 1990s."

"I don't think I'm asking people to believe," Lynda Tillman said. "What I ask is that they simply keep their minds open to the possibility. I think the evidence will take care of the rest."

As he typed up Lynda Tillman's words, Mitchell had to admit that she was a complex one. Not a fraud—at least not intentionally. Self-conned, maybe. Believed it herself, though her demeanor struck him as somehow too sensible and down-to-earth for that. People were always full of contradictions. Just look at him: everything else in his home was the latest in high-tech, except this old manual typewriter that he pounded away on, the instrument through which he now made his living. He had his reasons though, he thought. He glanced at the picture of himself and his wife, then back to the TV.

"We thought it might be fun to share that evidence with my second guest," the host continued, lifting up a book to show its title to the audience—a gesture Mitchell heartily approved of. "He's a physicist-turned-debunker and author of the new book, *Psychic Phenomena: A*

Rational Perspective. Please welcome Mr. Leviticus Mitchell."

Mitchell watched himself step out onto the set as the host and Lynda Tillman stood and applauded his entrance. On the screen he didn't seem nearly as uncomfortable as he'd felt—actually looked a bit cocky in what he thought of as his "Carl Sagan togs," black collarless sweater-shirt offset by suitcoat and slacks. He shook hands with the host and with Lynda Tillman, who looked almost as surprised on TV now as she had during the taping. Clearly, the producers had not informed her that she would be appearing with a skeptical scientist.

"So, Mr. Mitchell, why this calling?" the host asked. "Why a debunker, refuting the claims of the paranormal?"

"I became aware of the harm that irrational beliefs can cause for the layperson and I wanted to do something about it," Mitchell said on the TV. "And I guess I got bored sitting in a lab."

The line got the expected laugh. Typing, Mitchell felt both gratified and embarrassed. There had been so much more to his decision than that. His wife's death had affected him in many ways, some as simple as his using this typewriter. Carrie had been a computer consultant and using a word processor somehow felt like too much a reminder of her, ever since her death.

Some of the effects, though, had been as profound as his decision to give up his professorship in physics, after he had spent all those years in graduate school training for that very role. Carrie's death had made him realize that life was too short to spend on doing anything to which he was less than one hundred percent committed. He had only been an assistant professor a very few years when he realized what a drain his teaching had already become. Even his scholarship was becoming distinctly second tier. The inevitable mathematics had grown beyond him. Doing top work in mathematical physics, he began to realize, was a young man's game.

Carrie's death had called it all into question, right at the front of his mind. Better to take the skills he'd developed and apply them where they'd still be useful than just take up space in the lab, teaching undergraduates year after year, always different yet always the same, and always the ungrateful numbering far too many among them.

"—why don't we run the video that Lynda took of her alleged ghost," the talk show host continued from the TV, "and let you do a little on-the-fly debunking for us?"

Mitchell barely heard the second part of the host's taped intro, for during it his doorbuzzer began to sound, loudly and insistently. He jumped up from his desk and headed toward the door. Behind him, the talk show host yammered on as Lynda Tillman's "ghost video" began to play on the screen.

"Lynda, why don't you narrate for us?"

"Well, this image was taken at approximately 11:15 in the evening," Lynda said unsteadily, first over grainy video imagery of the interior of an old house, then describing an amorphous whitish shape moving along one wall. "I shot it in an abandoned house not far from where I live. I was completely alone at the time when I felt this presence—"

"Yes—?" Mitchell said as he approached the entry.

He opened the door and was astounded to see Lynda Tillman, the very woman talking on TV, now standing before him—in his doorway and in the flesh.

"You?" Mitchell asked, too stunned for social graces. "What are you doing here?"

Lynda Tillman, however, noting what was playing on the TV, said nothing—just stalked further into the room, her eyes focused on the screen.

"We're most likely just looking at a flare in the lens," Mitchell speculated from the TV.

"A flare in the lens?" Lynda heard herself say on television. "Don't you need a light source for that to happen?"

"Yes," Mitchell replied on screen, "but the moon is a strong enough source—"

"Hey, what do you think you're doing?" Mitchell asked from behind her, back by the door. "I really don't have time to speak with you right now."

Lynda glanced back at Mitchell, who stood dressed in jeans and a trendy "Capitalism Is Organized Crime" t-shirt. The brash rationalist, in casual mode.

"Too busy admiring your performance?" Lynda asked disdainfully as the TV show continued to play on in the background behind them.

"I was transcribing the interview for an upcoming book, if you must know," Mitchell said. "Now I'm going to have to ask you to leave."

"Look, you have a standing offer of five thousand

dollars to anyone who can prove the existence of the supernatural," Lynda said, walking still further into the room. "Isn't that right?"

"Yes, yes I do," Mitchell said with a wry shrug. "But do you have any idea how many people have made a try for that money?"

Lynda pulled an envelope from the pocket of her suit jacket.

"How many people have offered you the five thousand, Mitchell?"

"Are you kidding?" Mitchell asked, absently picking up the remote control for the TV.

"There's something I didn't mention on that stupid talk show, Mitchell," Lynda said levelly. "That ghost—the ghost you believe was a lens flare—I believe it's my son."

In the silence that opened between them, the background noise of the TV interview seemed to swell up intrusively.

"What you mean," Lynda said on TV, "is that it has to be anything but a ghost, since ghosts don't fit into your framework."

"My only 'framework'," the TV Mitchell said with an edge in his voice, "is science. I apply the rigors of science to my observations of the real world."

In that real world now, Mitchell thumbed off the TV via remote. Politeness couldn't hurt, he supposed. He invited Ms. Tillman to sit down, and asked her if she'd like a drink. She muttered something about how she'd just started drinking again, and asked for a scotch. Mitchell went to the kitchen to pour each of them a glass of straight Chivas.

"Why are you so sure your son is dead?" Mitchell asked as he poured the drinks. Before the interview he had done a little background research on Ms. Tillman, under the heading of "Know Thy Enemy." She had divorced her husband a couple of years back, and her son Derek had recently gone missing—a runaway, according to the papers. "I mean, most parents of missing children believe their kids are alive somewhere."

She joined him in the kitchen and he handed her a drink.

"I guess I'm a little short on that kind of faith," she said, sipping her scotch. "I keep hearing his voice."

"What do you mean?" Mitchell asked, his curiosity roused almost despite himself. "When?"

"The first time was in that house," she said, glancing up from her drink. "The same one in that video I took. It's been deserted for years. I'd heard that Derek used to go out there sometimes—to be by himself. You know how teenage kids are."

Mitchell nodded, but said nothing.

"After Derek disappeared," Lynda Tillman continued, "the police checked the house out and didn't find anything. They think Derek ran away from home, but I know better." She shrugged and looked back down into her drink, as if answers might be found there. "Anyway, I didn't have anywhere else to look. So I went to the house."

Mitchell noticed a hesitancy in her voice.

"Go on," he said, trying to sound encouraging.

Lynda took a sip of her scotch before continuing.

"I was walking through the place," she said, her eyes staring off into the middle distance of memory, "when I started to hear a sound. At first I thought it was the wind—you know, a tree brushing up against a wall or something. But the sound became louder. Clearer. It was Derek's voice. Calling for me. I ran through the house, looking for him, but he wasn't there, just his voice." She fought back the tears welling up in her eyes. "Oh God—his voice! It sounded like he was dying, like he was being killed in that house!"

Mitchell set down his scotch.

"Ms. Tillman," he began, trying to sound fair but also firm, "when the mind undergoes the type of stress associated with the loss of a loved one, it can often manufacture illusions—"

"'—so real they can seem like supernatural entities,'" Lynda said in a voice of mingled pain and disdain. "I've read Chapter Three in your latest book."

Mitchell sighed.

"Why don't you tell me exactly what it is you want?"

"I want you to go to that house with me."

"Why?" Mitchell asked, glancing around his tastefully furnished apartment, finding a certain comfort in its overall order and symmetry—a comfort he happened to need just now, given the personally painful direction this conversation was taking.

Lynda put down her drink and came closer to him

before she spoke. Even Mitchell could see that what she was about to say was not easy for her, almost as if she knew how crazy it was going to sound.

"I believe my son's spirit is somehow—trapped—inside that house."

"Look," Mitchell began, trying to appear understanding but definitely feeling out of his depth. "I'm not—"

"You're the only one I can count on," Lynda said, so plaintively yet so urgently that he didn't know whether she was going to grab him by the shirt collar or cry on his shoulder. She did neither. "If I'm right, I want to know that. If I'm crazy, then I want to know that. I need you."

She pressed the envelope with the money into his hands. He stared at her, confused.

"From my divorce settlement," she said. "What's left of it anyway."

"You can't possibly afford to part with this," Mitchell said, staring down at the envelope, knowing it held ready cash, at least a quarter of what he was making from the advance on his next book, and for a lot less effort, most likely.

"I can't afford not to part with it," Lynda said firmly.

She downed the remainder of her scotch. Mitchell considered her offer a long moment, then gave the envelope back to her. For a moment she thought Mitchell was rejecting her offer, and that must have shown in her eyes.

"Hold onto it," Mitchell said, "until we're finished."

Crossing the border from Canada into the U.S. as he followed Lynda in her car, Mitchell felt the way he always did—full of both wistful yearning and resolute acceptance—whenever he re-entered the country of his birth. An American expatriate since fleeing the draft during the latter days of the Vietnam War, he was part of a community of such expatriates living in Vancouver.

By and large they were a successful bunch. One of them had even achieved a measure of international fame as the leading light of a new generation of science fiction writers. Mitchell had been a science fiction fan in his youth—before Canada, college, and career had devoured all his time. In his mind, America, science fiction, and his own lost youth were all of a piece, as was the nostalgia he felt for each of them.

Ahead, Lynda in her vintage Buick exited the freeway for the surface streets of Bellingham, Washington. Mitchell followed her to the driveway of her modest home at the edge of town, where she parked her car before joining him in his Jeep. Mitchell driving, they headed out of town, onto roads that got smaller and more wooded with every mile.

"Abrams, the original owner of the house, disappeared about six years ago," Lynda said as they got closer to their destination.

"Disappeared?"

"Yeah," Lynda said, nodding. "Took folks a few

weeks to figure it out, since he didn't come out much anyway. According to the papers, he just left everything behind. Hasn't been heard from since."

On a rise before them, a boarded-up and clearly abandoned mansion in the Queen Anne style hove into view against a background of dark pine forest. Someone had apparently, without much real thought, thrown up a cheap split fence and staple-gunned NO TRESPASSING and FOR SALE signs to it.

Mitchell pulled his Jeep over to the side of the road, and he and Lynda climbed out into the cloudy midmorning light. Staring at the boarded-up Queen Anne—complete with tower—he had to admit that it certainly fit the part.

Lynda glanced at him and he was struck—not for the first time—by the woman's strong, intelligent good looks.

"Well, sure looks haunted," he said, to distract them both from his own stare. "You know how to pick 'em. I'll give you that much."

Too late he caught himself, realizing again how seriously Lynda was taking all this. It was her son who was missing, after all. Mitchell remained silent as she led him toward a gap in the fence, then on up through the weed-choked and branch-littered front lawn toward the front door. Overhead a crow called in the overcast sky and a train whistle sounded in the distance.

Mitchell had to push heavily against the front door. Apparently the house had settled, making the door prone to sticking. Daylight fell through open slats in the boarded-up windows, spilling slabs of dusty light onto the floors and walls. Standing in the foyer, Mitchell took in the empty-house graffiti, the battered and peeling walls, the general webs and tatters of decay. He coughed in the dust they'd stirred up on entering.

"I'll show you where it was," Lynda said, stepping through the foyer, moving through a hall toward what appeared to be a door to the basement. The floorboards creaked underfoot as Mitchell followed her.

She opened the door and together they made their way down the steps leading into the basement, Mitchell shining a penlight into the gloomy half-light before them. Near the bottom of the steps a bare incandescent bulb hung from the ceiling at just above head level, its on/off pull-string dangling down. Out of reflex Mitchell pulled the light cord several times, though consciously he knew that the power to this place had to have been off for years.

"It was about here that I heard it," Lynda said, hugging herself in her sweater against the damp cold of the basement.

"The screams?" Mitchell asked, flashing the penlight into the basement gloom.

"Yes."

"What time of day was that?" he asked as they began to move further into the basement.

"About this time," Lynda replied. "Why?"

"Southern Pacific line runs not too far from here," Mitchell said, still flashing his penlight among the columns and walls and discarded furniture of the basement. "According to their timetables, freights pass and—"

"It wasn't a train," Lynda said grumpily. "I know

what a train sounds like."

"Shh," Mitchell said, concentrating. "Listen."

Both of them strained to hear. For a beat there seemed to be nothing, then something became audible—though what was hard to say. A high-pitched sound, not quite rhythmic, rather like someone calling out or even screaming from a great distance.

"That's what I heard," Lynda said. Mitchell nodded and began moving purposefully about the basement. He slowed beside, then walked past a heating oil tank, as if trying to locate the source of the sound, which now was intermittently accompanied by clanks as well. Slowly Lynda followed him.

Mitchell stopped beside a pleated metal duct coming off the furnace.

"Have you ever heard of Occam's razor?" Mitchell asked, turning toward Lynda.

"No," she said, not much enjoying his condescending tone.

"It's an axiom," Mitchell continued, rather pedantically, "which states that the simplest theory is usually the correct one."

With an offhand flourish he separated the loose ductwork from the furnace. The shrieking wind sounds abruptly stopped. The look he gave Lynda was more than a bit on the smug side. Lynda frowned and turned away, walking back upstairs to the deserted kitchen. Mitchell followed.

"Take my advice, Lynda," he said when he had joined her in the kitchen. "If you want to find out what happened to your son—"

"Listen—" Lynda said. With a soft whoosh a wind

came up out of nowhere, an abrupt puff that mussed up their hair, then receded like something Doppler-shifting away. Now it was Lynda's turn to look smug.

"Maybe you'd better check those train schedules, Mitchell."

"That?" Mitchell said with a laugh, moving around the room with sudden animation. "That's called a draft! You get those in drafty houses. The so-called Fort Wayne poltergeist back in '81 turned out to be an open window in the attic."

Then, almost as an afterthought, the entire house seemed to shift a millimeter, like some enormous living thing adjusting to a more comfortable position in sleep. A voice called out from somewhere in the house, airy and hard to place, coming from nowhere and everywhere at once. To Lynda's ears the voice, for all its reverberant ubiquity, was clearly saying one word: "Mom."

Pale, she stared at Mitchell, who had definitely heard it too and was doing a rather poor job of trying to hide his bewilderment.

"I'll need a couple of hours," he said shakily, "to get some equipment."

~~~~~~~~~~

Back at his home in Vancouver, he gathered his gear—a pair of kerosene lamps, a video camera, a small seismograph, and a temperature gauge. As he was getting ready to lock up, though, he lost his argument with himself and decided the "Abrams

Haunting" just might merit the use of his most expensive piece of debunking equipment: a portable within-pulse electronic sector-scanning sonar array, his pride and joy.

Once everything was loaded into his Jeep, Mitchell headed back across the border to meet with Lynda and head back to the Abrams place for their "stake-out" that evening. On the way, though, the notion of a stake-out got him thinking of the police and he decided to stop at the police station and do a little more background legwork.

After talking with a receiving officer, he was introduced to Sergeant Roth almost immediately. A man in his mid-forties with a used-car salesman's thick shock of slightly over-groomed hair and a suit and tie to match the look, Roth nonetheless seemed measured and reasonable. The sergeant glanced absently at a file folder as the two made their way through the ringing phones and dispatcher drone of a small city's crowded main police station.

"You're that psychic, aren't you?" Roth asked.

"No!" Mitchell said quickly as he followed the shorter man through the thronged corridors of the station. "I'm not a psychic."

"Wait a sec—" Roth said, glancing at Mitchell without breaking stride, taking in his jeans and leather coat and longish brown hair. "You're the scientist. I saw you on TV with that Tillman woman. You really put her in her place."

They came into the squad room, Roth heading for the file cabinets behind his desk.

"So what brings you here?"

"Ms. Tillman," Mitchell said, clearing his throat, "hired me to help locate her son."

Roth gave Mitchell a long look. A goateed young officer at a desk nearby—named Gould, judging by the nameplate on the edge of the blotter—smirked broadly.

"Come again?" Roth asked.

"It's a long story," Mitchell said, hoping to shift the conversation in a more fruitful direction. "Look, can you tell me anything about Derek Tillman?"

"Probably nothing you don't already know," Roth said, opening the file cabinet and putting away the file he'd been carrying. "We haven't found him, but we've got a pretty good hunch that he's okay."

"Why's that?" Mitchell persisted.

"One week before Derek was reported missing," Roth said, shutting the file drawer, "he and his mom had the mother of all arguments. She slapped him pretty hard."

Mitchell pondered that as Roth sat down at his desk, his back to the scientist.

"Over what?"

"She didn't tell you?" Roth asked.

"No."

Roth traded a knowing look with Gould.

"Ms. Tillman didn't like who her boy was seeing at the time," Gould put in. "A young girl who 'disappeared' about the same time as Derek. Nadia Torrance—nothing but trouble. We think they took off together."

Mitchell glanced back toward Roth.

"Where are her parents?"

"In Los Angeles," Roth said, glancing up from the report he was filling out on his desk. "They could give a hoot in hell about their daughter's whereabouts, though. If I were you, I'd take the same attitude, Mr. Mitchell. There's very little you can do here."

Mitchell thanked them and left the police station. Driving to Ms. Tillman's, Mitchell thought about what the police had said and considered how best to broach the subject with Lynda. When he arrived at her house, though, there was no time for that, since she greeted him with blankets and sleeping bags for their little sleep-over at the Abrams place.

By the time they got to the decrepit house, the moon had started to rise into a strangely quiet night. Once inside, though, they decided to fill the silence and solitude with activity, setting up the lamps and camera and monitor and seismograph, then rolling out the blankets and sleeping bags. Adjusting his video display hookup, Mitchell figured it was as good a time as any to bring up what he'd learned from the police.

"I stopped at the police station on the way back," Mitchell said, watching horizontal rolls on the monitor. "They said you got into quite an argument with your son before he disappeared."

"You what?" Lynda asked, incredulous.

"I went to the police," Mitchell said, noting her look. "Background research. It's the same thing psychics do to get info on clients for readings.... Well?"

Lynda stopped toying with the dangling lens cap of the still camera on the tripod beside her. She shifted position where she sat on the arm of an old and battered sofa.

"We did have a fight," she said at last.

"About the girl?" Mitchell asked as he came toward her to check the image in the viewfinder of the still camera.

"Yeah," Lynda said, glancing toward him, then away, into her own memories. "Nadia was a screwed-up kid. I didn't want Derek seeing her. You want a drink?"

Mitchell looked up from the viewfinder to see Lynda pulling a flask from her bag, along with two paper cups.

"Thanks," Mitchell said, watching as she poured liquor into the two cups, then taking the one she offered him.

"Anyway, this girl did drugs," Lynda continued, "and she was trying to get Derek into them too."

Mitchell sipped and sloshed the scotch around in the cup.

"And after you had this fight with your son," he said, "that's when he disappeared, along with Nadia."

"Yes," she said, a defensive tone creeping into her voice. She knew where Mitchell was going with this. She'd thought about it herself, long since.

"And you still think Derek's spirit is in this house," Mitchell said, definitely not as a question.

"I guess you can just call it a matter of faith," Lynda replied, raising her cup and drinking.

"Faith?" Mitchell said with a laugh as he walked over to grab up some of his tracking and monitoring gear. "That's just another way of saying there's no proof."

"Have you always been such a nonbeliever?" Lynda asked.

"Believe so," Mitchell said, not unaware of the flippancy of his response.

"That's not what I understand," Lynda said, rather inscrutably, then paused to take another sip of her drink. "After your wife died, you visited a few psychics yourself."

Mitchell stared at her in absolute surprise.

"Background research," she deadpanned, responding to Mitchell's look. "One thing I don't know, though, is why you became a skeptic."

Mitchell tried to laugh it off at first, but Lynda's look told him that she genuinely wanted to know. He gulped down the remainder of his drink, uncomfortable with delving into this part of his past.

"During a séance," he began, clearing his throat, "I caught a medium faking my wife's voice. Oh, she really had me going—until she called me 'Levi'. My wife never called me 'Levi'. Hated the name. She always called me 'Mitchell', and that was just fine with me. I wasn't too fond of 'Leviticus' as a first name myself. Anyway, I saw the whole psychic and séance thing for what it was: a stage show, cooked up for people who can't face the reality of death."

Lynda looked at him with the most penetrating eyes. Mitchell felt naked in her gaze.

"I take it you don't believe in an afterlife?" she asked.

"I've never seen any evidence for one," he said, then put down his cup. "I grew up in a hard-shell Baptist household in up-holler Virginia. How do you think I got named 'Leviticus'? Book of laws and faith, rules and belief. I learned the laws and rules of science, though. That got me past my upbringing, got me out of those shotgun-shack hills. I've been pretty much inoculated against religious mystification ever since."

"So where do you believe your wife is?" Lynda asked, without cruelty.

"In the ground," Mitchell said, his voice tinged with bitterness. "Just so much dust. Like everyone else who's died throughout human history. The sooner we accept that, the sooner we can get on with our lives after someone we love passes on."

Lynda finished her drink and set it aside.

"But in one way," she said quietly, "you haven't gone on with your life. You're still alone."

A silence opened between them. Her words had clearly struck a chord in both of them. At an even deeper level, they had come perilously close to speaking something yet unspoken between the two of them, something about the two of them—something about which they were not yet ready to speak.

"Lots of lives are lived alone," Mitchell said, staring down at the floor from where he leaned against a wall. "They're still lives."

~~~~~~~~~~~~~~~

By the time Mitchell had arrayed against the night his full armamentarium of science—video, seismic, and sonar—it had grown quite late. They had, between the two of them, killed off the flask of scotch Lynda had brought with her. The video monitor showed an image of the broken-banistered staircase like a scene from a late-night horror movie stuck in freeze frame. On the couch in the living room, Lynda was already more or less asleep and Mitchell was slipping off in that same direction when he thought he heard something—a rustling, a clatter of bottles, maybe even a footstep or a window slamming down in the basement.

Coming fully awake, he grabbed up a heavy high-powered flashlight from beside one of the kerosene lamps and headed toward the basement. Making his way down the basement steps, he shone the flashlight before him into the darkness. Off in one corner of the basement he thought he heard a sound and headed toward it.

"Mom!"

Upstairs, Lynda had just come fully awake.

"MOM!"

Lynda got to her feet and headed slowly toward where one of the kerosene lamps burned.

"Help me!" said the ubiquitous, reverberant voice—clotted, raspy, but still recognizably Derek's. "Help me! Get me out!"

The voice seemed to be coming most loudly from upstairs, on the second floor. Lynda started up the stairs, kerosene lamp in hand.

In the basement, Mitchell found that one of the basement windows was now open, when he could have sworn it had been closed, earlier. He shone the light out the window, down the hill toward his Jeep. For a moment he thought he saw someone—a long-haired figure in a ratted wool sweater, standing near a tree—but when he swung the light back there was no one there. Probably nothing, he thought. Or at worst a transient. He'd heard that they often squatted in abandoned buildings.

Lynda, meanwhile, had reached the second floor. The raspy, reverberant voice was louder now, more insistent.

"Mom!"

"Derek?" she called, continuing further down the hallway. Beneath her feet the floorboards and wainscoting creaked like the planks of a ship at sea. For a moment there was silence.

"Get me out!" said the voice. It seemed to be coming from somewhere down the hallway, directly in front of her. She shone her lantern there, right up against the wall, but she saw nothing. She turned and looked back up the hall, toward the landing from which she'd come, but a scuttling sound—sudden and immense—made her turn round again.

In the light of the lantern the wall before her was now liquid, pulsing, bubbling like a pot of soup on slow boil. Out of the boiling wall a face emerged, then part of a torso—Derek, without his glasses, composed somehow of the very fabric of the building.

"Mom!" said the ghostly figure, reaching his arm out of the wall, grabbing toward her. "Help! Get me out!"

"Derek!" Lynda screamed, reaching out like a mother but in the same instant backing up like a shocked and very scared human being, pure fright overcoming maternal instinct as she moved back toward the stairs.

"Mom! Help! Help!" the ghostly figure of Derek shrieked as his form began to disappear again, as if the wall were sucking him back down into itself.

"Derek! Derek!" Lynda screamed and cried, still backing up, until she felt herself miss a step behind her. Falling through the air backwards, too late she realized she had stepped back onto the staircase . . . .

"Lynda?"

A voice seemed to call her from far away. She opened her eyes and sprang up with a start, but it wasn't a ghost. It was Mitchell, seated on the couch beside her.

"What happened?" she asked, noting vaguely that morning light was coming in through the windows, and that she was stretched out on the couch under a blanket.

"When I came up from the basement," Mitchell said, "I found you on the floor at the foot of the stairs. Out cold. You've been sleeping ever since. Too much to drink, I think."

It all began coming back to her.

"You didn't see it?" she asked, disappointed.

"See what?"

"It was Derek," she said, agitated. "Oh God, Mitchell—upstairs, he was in the walls—"

"In the walls?" he asked, disbelief strong in his voice.

"The wall changed into him," she insisted, trying to explain it to herself, too. "Like he was part of the house—"

"I checked my instruments," Mitchell said, glancing away from her. "There was some activity on the seismograph, but it could've been a passing truck."

Frustrated, Lynda flicked the blanket off her and swung her legs to the floor.

"You've got a real thing about transportation, don't you?" she said, peeved. "Everything's either trains or trucks—"

She stood up unsteadily, breathing hard, and started to stumble.

"Take it easy," Mitchell said, grabbing her arm to steady her. "Take it easy. Are you okay?"

"Derek's spirit is in this house," Lynda said resolutely, walking slowly round the couch. "I think it's trying to tell me something. What happened to him—"

Mitchell let out a sigh of frustration, then set off purposefully for the foyer.

"I'm gonna clear this up once and for all," he called back as he left the room.

When Mitchell returned from the foyer, he was

carrying on his shoulder a large instrument similar in overall size and shape to a large broadcast-quality video camera, but with numerous extra dials and readouts built into an oversized panel.

"What's that?" Lynda asked.

"A portable netsonde—an electronic sector-scanning sonar array," Mitchell said proudly. "It cost me most of the advance from my first book."

"You lost me after 'portable'," Lynda said.

"It utilizes the same principle commercial fishermen use to find schools of fish."

Mitchell switched it on. The device made a high-pitched hum.

"Are we going after bass or bluegill?" Lynda asked sarcastically.

"You said what you saw came out of the walls, right?" Mitchell asked, looking through the netsonde at lines of pixels tracing the various layers of building material on a heads-up video display. While Lynda watched he sighted along the walls. "Well, this can tell what's behind the walls. Now where'd you say you saw it?"

"Upstairs."

They started upstairs, Mitchell staring through the viewer on the way up.

"Nothing . . . nothing," he said, then turned it off when he saw Lynda give him a dirty look.

On the second floor, Lynda gestured toward a space on the wall.

"Here," she said. "This is where I saw it."

Mitchell switched it on again—the same annoying, high-pitched hum.

"I see a wall," he said. "I see a big wall."

"Okay, Mitchell. Very funny. You've made your point. But I don't know what this proves."

"We don't know what it proves," Mitchell said, staring at the video-readout on the array, "until we're . . . . Wait a sec—"

"What is it?" Lynda asked.

"Let me tighten the beam width," Mitchell said. "There's something here."

"What?"

"With this resolution it's hard to say with certainty," he said, "but I could swear it's a door."

Lynda stared at him when he glanced away from the netsonde's video readout.

"Why cover it up?" she asked.

Mitchell put the netsonde on the floor, aimed at the line of the hidden doorjamb, then headed downstairs. Lynda followed him to the base of the stairs.

"That's what we're going to find out," he said, jogging toward the front door. "I've got a wrecking bar in the Jeep. I'm pretty sure it'll go through a door, or lath and plaster."

When Mitchell came back in the house, he had a long heavy crowbar held in both hands across the front of his torso. Lynda led the way upstairs. Mitchell quickly got into position and began banging and ramming away at the line of the hidden doorjamb, prying into the space between door and wall. Chunks of wood and plaster flew everywhere in the upstairs hallway. From time to time Mitchell stopped, and he and Lynda peeled away layers of wallpaper and shoveled out shattered plaster with their hands. The vigorous, dirty work made them thankful for the cool October weather.

Pausing to wipe plaster dust from her brow, Lynda could have sworn that she saw a dribble of clear viscous ooze slip down from the hole they were opening up. She blinked and it was gone. No liquid could disappear that fast. Must have been a dust mote in her eye. Mitchell, who was breaking through the wall with more vigor than she might have expected of him, had now cleared a hole large enough for them to squeeze in through. Seeing that the space inside was dark, she went downstairs to grab the heavy-duty flashlight.

Mitchell was already squeezing into the darkened room beyond when she shone the flashlight in behind him. Lynda handed the flashlight to him, then squeezed into the room herself. The room seemed about as large as a good-sized master bedroom, though it gave off a stale chemical smell more appropriate to an old garage. Along the walls, glassware—test tubes and beakers and other refugees from high school chem-lab classes—glimmered in the flashlight's beam, shrouded in cobwebs. Mitchell was taking an extremely keen interest in the shrouded glassware and grime-covered equipment.

"I'll be damned," he said. "Burettes, stoppered flasks, an autoclave, a rectifier, diffusion pump, desiccator, condensor—"

"What is all this stuff?" Lynda asked, looking

about at the gear and its rough metal shelving.

Mitchell looked at her, thoughtful. "This is a laboratory," he said.

"A laboratory?" she asked, waving away some dusty webbing from before her face.

"Biochemistry setup," Mitchell elaborated, "and very professional, too."

Lynda made her way slowly about the lab. She had hoped to get away from the stale chemical smell, but that clearly wasn't possible.

"What was Abrams doing with a laboratory in his house?" she asked. "Why would he cover it up?"

"Your guess is as good as mine," he remarked, heading over toward her with the flashlight. "Well, maybe not as good—especially if I'd thought to investigate the background of this house's last owner, instead of just yours and your son's."

"Don't kick yourself too hard," she said, continuing to make her way through the deep dust of the lab. "Even the pope of science can make a mistake . . . . Mitchell, what's this?"

Lynda stood before a large container—almost a chamber—of sealed plexiglas, the size of a large aquarium. Mitchell shone the light toward the plexiglas chamber as he came closer. Inside was a melon-sized, dark-gray, pockmarked rock affixed to a stainless steel rack. One side was smooth, as if it had been sheared off from a larger chunk.

"What is that? Lynda asked, looking at the rock in the glare of Mitchell's flashlight.

"Obviously the center of attention, judging from

the layout of the lab," Mitchell replied, playing the beam around the surface of the rock. "Looks like it might be feldspar, or breccia."

"Should I know what that is? Lynda asked, a bit peeved at the jargon.

"Very common material," he said, engrossed by they find, "particularly in meteorites."

~~~~~~~~~~

The two of them spent a good portion of the rest of the day making the hole in the wall bigger, then bringing the entire plexiglas chamber down the stairs, out the door and into the back of the Jeep. Lynda thought it was strangely like furniture moving, with Mitchell treating the plexiglas container and its rock as if together they made up some prized antique.

Then they drove north. Mitchell was ready to answer any question the border guard might pose them, but the Canadian official seemed uninterested as he waved them through. They drove on to Sheffield University, where Mitchell had held his last teaching position and where he apparently still maintained some connection with the labs.

The nature of that connection both surprised Lynda and struck her as all too predictable. The lab tech who came to help them with their find was named Jennifer. An attractive woman in her late twenties, Jennifer was a former student of Mitchell's, with whom he was entirely too flirtatious, as far as Lynda was concerned.

Otherwise, though, Jennifer seemed quite professional, quickly decanting the rock into a large glove-box enclosure. She adeptly sawed the stone into neat halves, commenting on its "unexpected hollowness" and "almost geode-like interior." Watching from the other side of the glove-boxed chamber, Lynda said nothing. This was Mitchell and Jennifer's show.

"It's mildly radioactive," Jennifer said, running some kind of Geiger counter over the split stone, "but no more than twelve millirems."

"See the micro-impact scoring?" Mitchell said from over Jennifer's shoulder, in a mentorly fashion.

"Could be a meteorite," Jennifer agreed, "or a chunk of one. Where did you get this?"

"A fellow named Abrams had it," Mitchell said, perhaps a bit embarrassed. "I'll fill you in later. Right now, how about running a few tests?"

"Anything for a former professor," Jennifer said with a smile, pulling her arms out of the glove-box's gauntlets.

"Knew I could count on you," Mitchell said, putting his hand on her shoulder in a comradely fashion. "Give me a Liebig, and put it through the Duboscq too, okay? And if it's anorthosite, you might want to do some polarization runs on it. Lynda?"

She walked toward him and they started out of the lab.

"Hey," Jennifer said, putting her hands back into the heavy rubber gauntlets, "just be glad you gave me an A."

As they were leaving, Lynda saw that Jennifer had

picked up one of the stone halves in her gloved hands and was staring at its partially hollow interior. The image stuck with her as they drove back toward the Abrams place, stopping at a liquor store to pick up a bag of snack chips and a sixer of beer for Mitchell and a bottle of scotch for herself. She took a couple of hits on the bottle as they got closer to the Abrams house.

The moon was high by the time they reached the abandoned building. Mitchell jumped out of the car eagerly, Lynda following more slowly. He strode through the gate and up the rise, but she hesitated on the threshold of the yard, staring up at the moonlit house.

"Are you okay?" Mitchell asked, turning back toward her.

"It was about this time last night that I saw Derek," she said stonily.

"You don't have to go back in," Mitchell offered. "I can do this alone."

"No," she said, mustering her courage and starting forward. "I'm all right."

They entered the house, grabbed flashlights, and climbed the stairs to the site of their partial wall demolition. Inside the lab, they scoured everything with the beams from their flashlights. Mitchell peered into the centrifuge, checked under various pieces of equipment. Lynda opened a cabinet, finding stacks of Pyrex beakers and solution bottles inside. The bottles seemed to remind her of something and she sighed, taking out her flask-shaped bottle of scotch and stealing a sip. She turned to see Mitchell watching her.

"You like to drink, don't you?" he asked, crouching down, continuing to look—on the lower shelves, now—for whatever it was he was looking for.

"Believe it or not," Lynda said, "I was on the wagon for years, until I lost Derek. I think I've got cause to drink, and there are some things about me that are none of your business."

"Sorry."

Lynda capped the flask and spoke down toward Mitchell's backside and legs where he was rooting around in some stacks of lab trays.

"When I drink I don't dream," Lynda said. "When I don't dream, the next day's usually a pretty good one."

She pocketed the bottle. Just as she was about to ask Mitchell if he ever dreamed about his deceased wife, he called out.

"Wait!" he said. "Wait just a minute!"

He stood up and put what looked like a bound notebook on the shelf beside him, quickly bringing the flashlight to bear on its contents. The pages were densely covered with figures and formulas, and the notebook as a whole was stuffed with newspaper clippings.

"This looks like a combination diary and work notebook," Mitchell said. "Bingo!"

They returned downstairs to the couch, divvying up the material, Mitchell poring over the work notes and Lynda looking through the news clippings. Splitting the bag of snack chips between the two of them, each became totally engrossed, giving little reports now and then when something in their reading struck one or the other of them as interesting.

"Says here that Abrams was a senior scientist at

Genedyne Biochemical," Lynda said, "and that Genedyne was closed by the EPA for an 'undetermined reason'."

Lynda held out the clipping she had just started reading. Mitchell took it from her. The headline read FEDERAL GOVERNMENT CLOSES GENEDYNE. In a related story on the same page was a photo of a bespectacled man in his forties—Abrams—and a subhead stating LOCAL SCIENTIST CITED IN EPA PROBE OF FIRM. Mitchell scanned the article, taking a swig off the bottle of beer in his other hand as he did.

"Abrams was under investigation," Mitchell said, puzzled.

"Does the article give a reason?"

"Doesn't say," Mitchell replied, putting down the beer and taking up the notebook again.

"Any clues in there?" Lynda asked, gesturing toward the notebook.

"Too many," Mitchell said. "There are references to material by several people: Svante Arrhenius, Lovecraft, Francis Crick, Weber and Greenberg, Hoyle and Wickramasinghe—"

"Who are they?" Lynda asked, continuing to look through the clippings.

"Well," Mitchell said, thoughtfully, "Arrhenius got the Nobel Prize—for Chemistry, I believe—back around the turn of the century. He predicted the greenhouse effect from burning fossil fuels—a full century ago. Crick is part of Watson and Crick, the DNA decoder gods. He's a Nobel laureate too. Hoyle's an astronomer, best known for advocating the idea of a steady state universe. I think

Wickramasinghe's his protégé or collaborator. I don't know who Weber and Greenberg are, particularly, but judging from these references I'm fairly certain they're part of the scientific community. Lovecraft was a pulp writer, mostly wrote this strange hybrid stuff that was part horror and part science fiction. I read his stuff in reprint collections when I was a teenager. I think Hoyle wrote science fiction, too."

"Anything link them all together?" Lynda asked, taking another sip of scotch.

"I'm not sure," Mitchell said, nursing his beer. "When Abrams mentions any of them in his notes it's like he's invoking some kind of grand tradition. Something keeps scratching at the back of my brain telling me I know how they're connected, but I just can't piece it together."

"How about Abrams's other notes?" Lynda asked.

"Not much help," Mitchell said, shaking his head. "His experimental remarks are pretty cryptic and specialized: 'I will attempt to introduce a longer stacking element, a biphenyl instead of naphthalene, to induce an autocatalytic reaction.' Stuff like that."

"It'll never make the *New York Times* bestseller list," Lynda said wryly.

"That it won't," Mitchell said, going back to his reading.

Lynda looked at Mitchell closely, for a considerable time. He was too wrapped up in reading the notebook to notice her stare.

"So how come you never remarried?" she asked.

"Hmmm?" Mitchell asked, so lost in his notes that he'd only distantly heard what she'd asked.

"Never mind," Lynda said, just a bit too quickly. Mitchell looked up.

"Sorry," he said, looking from her to the notes and back, "It's just that none of this is making any sense."

"Not everything makes sense."

"I don't accept that," Mitchell said, shaking his head dismissively as he returned his gaze to the notes.

"Maybe that's why it's so hard for you to believe in anything," Lynda speculated. "With you, everything has to have a reason, a formula."

"Everything does have a formula," Mitchell said positively. "In fact, I'm looking at a whole page of them at this very instant."

"What about love?" Lynda asked. A risky question, but she had to ask it.

"Hormonal secretions that stimulate certain sensory-pleasure regions of the brain," he said, half-seriously, rather enjoying playing the part of the scientific pedant.

Lynda laughed aloud.

"I'll bet your wife loved to hear that over a candlelight dinner."

"We never had any candlelight dinners," Mitchell said, his tone changing despite his pretense of being deeply buried in the notes.

"Why am I not surprised?" Lynda asked, missing the change in his tone.

"It wasn't me," Mitchell said soberly. "Carrie just wasn't into fancy occasions."

Lynda recognized the shift in tone this time, and responded to it.

"What'd she like to do?" she asked, eating another chip as she put aside the news clippings.

"Camping. Canoeing," Mitchell said, smiling as if at a good memory. "Computing was strictly a nine-to-five thing with her. She was an outdoorswoman, really. I've never understood why the hell she married a scientist who practically lived in his lab."

"I can guess why," Lynda said.

"Oh yeah?" Mitchell asked, glancing up from the notes, adjusting his position slightly on the couch.

"Intelligence is sexy," Lynda said, "for some women."

"I don't know," Mitchell said with a shrug, trying to burrow back into the notes.

"What happened to her, Mitchell?"

He snapped the notebook shut, harder and more loudly than he'd intended.

"You don't have to tell me," Lynda said, backpedalling.

"Car accident," Mitchell gritted out. "Kid driving too fast. Ran a red light."

"I'm sorry," Lynda said, moved by the pain the recollection caused him.

"Yeah . . . ."

Lynda pulled out a beer, handed it to Mitchell. He opened it and took a good long pull.

Abruptly an unearthly groan and shriek sounded and Mitchell found plaster from the ceiling falling in his lap. He thought someone had driven a truck into the other side of the Abrams place—but no, this was something else. The house was undulating as if it were caught in the strong wave of a deep earthquake tremor.

Mitchell leapt to his feet and ran to his seismograph as the plaster continued to fall and the reverberant moaning and shrieking sounded everywhere. Even the most cursory glance at the seismic readout showed that this "quake" had a waveform signature unlike any seen before. What he saw when he looked up from the readout, however, was far more exotic and so unbelievable that he wondered if he might be losing his mind.

Faces in the walls, arms reaching out toward him.

"Derek! Nadia!" Lynda called out. "Mitchell, do you see?"

He saw, and heard. Trapped figures screaming to him for help, for release. Another visible form too, besides Derek and Nadia. A more ghostly and undefined presence—Abrams? or the memory of his shape?

Mitchell grabbed up the video camera from its tripod mount, swung around, and swiftly backed up to get a shot of the madness in front of him—too swiftly, for he went flipping backwards over the couch, knocking the lantern over to smash and breaking the connection for the light mounted on the videocam.

"Mitchell," Lynda said again, helping him up, "do you see?

Mitchell, though, was too busy trying to focus on the images in the walls to pay her much attention—able only to go on trying to dumbly record in the meager ambient light, his mind unable to process what he was seeing.

"This can't be happening," Mitchell said numbly.

The faces and arms abruptly began to recede into the wall and the moans and screams for help echoed off into the darkness. Now they had something else to worry about—shafts of bright light blasting through the boarded slats in the windows, around the front doorframe, through the keyhole.

"Mitchell—" Lynda said, grabbing him, both of them staring in amazement. The front door banged open and a figure stepped in—Officer Gould, in raid vest and cap, backed by other police officers in similar uniform.

"Party's over," Gould said loudly. "This area is now off limits."

~~~~~~~~~~~~~~~~

By the time they reached the police station, dawn was breaking in Bellingham. The story Mitchell and Lynda told the police so strained credulity that Roth and Gould demanded to see the video Mitchell had shot. Against his better judgment Mitchell put the videotape from his camera into a monitor/player in one of the police interrogation rooms and he and Lynda sat down at a conference table to watch it. Roth and Gould remained standing.

The tape turned out to be just as dark and grainy and handheld as Mitchell had feared. Impossible to really see anything—least of all "faces in the walls." The quality was even worse than Lynda's tape, the one he'd debunked on the talk show. Embarrassing.

Over by the door where Sergeant Roth and

Officer Gould watched the tape with them, Roth stood poker-faced, silent, occasionally sipping from a mug of coffee. Gould's sneer was almost audible in the room. Mercifully for Mitchell, the tape was coming to an end.

"Think it's dark enough?" Gould asked, trying to make his sarcasm sound like an innocent question.

"The lamp broke," Mitchell explained uncomfortably.

"I'm disappointed, Mitchell," Roth said, moving around toward the desk at the front of the room. "You of all people should be able to come up with something better than this."

"The tape's not important," Lynda said dismissively.

"She's right," Mitchell said, quick to agree. "I know what I saw."

"So what are you telling me?" Roth asked, leaning forward on the desk. "That the Abrams place is haunted?"

Mitchell found himself in an agonizingly uncomfortable position. He had sometimes wondered how his opposite numbers felt, believers being grilled by a skeptic. Now he knew.

"There's something there," Mitchell said awkwardly. "A presence—"

"A presence," Roth repeated, disbelief undeniable in his voice.

"All I know is that place is dangerous," Mitchell said, looking steadfastly at Roth, "and it should be sealed off."

Roth opened a drawer in the desk and reached inside.

"The Abrams house has been sealed off, and not because of any ghosts," Roth said confidently, removing something from the desk and walking toward Lynda. "The Abrams house is now a crime scene."

What Roth had removed from the desk was a small evidence bag, which he now placed on the table before Lynda Tillman. The bag held a twisted pair of wire-framed glasses.

"Do you recognize these, Ms. Tillman?"

Lynda studied them a moment, then bit down on her lip.

"They're—" she began, her voice quavering with emotion. "They look like Derek's."

"We think they are," Roth said with a brief nod as he snatched them back up.

"Where did you get them?" Mitchell asked, his scientific curiosity still very much online. By way of answer Roth ejected Mitchell's tape from the video monitor and popped in one of his own. An image came on: a transient in a ratted wool sweater and hooded sweatshirt, whom Mitchell could have sworn he'd seen somewhere before. Talking to a police interrogator. Mitchell and Lynda both tried to catch what the transient was saying, though at first it didn't sound like anything worth listening to, just a sparechangeman's mixed up alien-psychotic hypermantra.

"Consciousnesses within consciousnesses," the transient said rapidly, puffing determinedly on a cigarette and occasionally getting up to pace. "You see what I'm saying? It's all part of a whole. All part of one gigantic, all-encompassing scheme. We're nothing, you know? We're just servants, servants of twilight. The house is God, man, and you better not go messin' with the Lord. It ain't a mad vengeance kind of thing I'm talking about. God is coming—hell, he's already here—but he's not angry. He's hungry, like Jesus after forty days in the desert."

Roth pointed through the glass to an adjoining office, where the transient on the tape was sitting and gesticulating in the real world as a plainclothesman kept an eye on him.

"There's your 'presence', Mitchell," Roth said. "Luther Dobson. We ran him in for urinating in public. Claims he spent the night in the Abrams house. Claims Derek Tillman and Nadia Torrance are dead and buried inside the Abrams place."

Lynda got to her feet and walked slowly to the glass, her attention fixed on Dobson.

"We found your son's glasses on him," Roth said as Lynda walked past him. "Don't know if we can charge him with anything yet, though. He might have just found them. But we're not taking any chances."

Lynda lowered her head and turned away from the glass and the scene of Luther Dobson expostulating.

"We're going to start digging in the basement tomorrow," Roth continued. "You should go home, Mrs. Tillman. We'll call you if we find anything."

Fighting back strong emotion, Lynda left the room. Roth glowered at Mitchell.

"If you're taking advantage of a grieving, misguided

woman," Roth growled, "for some book or God knows what, I'll come down on you hard."

Mitchell was too stunned to respond. Roth stepped out of the room, leaving Gould behind with Mitchell.

"I heard the moans and shrieks coming from your 'haunted house,'" Gould said, insinuating lewdly. "Sounded more like the Tunnel of Love. We both know it ain't a book you're after, is it, Mitchell?"

"Go to hell," Mitchell said sharply. He had had enough.

"Don't believe in hell any more than you do," Gould said, stepping out of the room, into the waiting area beyond.

Mitchell was glad to leave, glad to be left alone at last. As he walked from the police station, part of him wanted to stop at Lynda's place so he could just talk with her. But no, he was still too overwrought, simultaneously exhausted and anxious from the way the night and morning had gone. He decided to drive back to Vancouver. Maybe by the time he got home he'd be tired enough to sleep, just take an afternoon nap.

When he got back to Vancouver, though, he was still too overtired to sleep. He had Abrams's notes in the Jeep, so to wind down further he decided to stop by the library and check out the works by Arrhenius and Crick and Hoyle and the rest that Abrams mentioned in his notebook.

By the time he left the library with an armload of books and photocopied articles, he was ready for that nap. He dropped the research material on the coffee table, dropped himself in his big armchair, and dropped immediately off to sleep.

He was awakened two hours later by the phone ringing. It was Lynda, already on the road on her way to see him. She was an hour out. He told her that he'd wait up for her.

Still exhausted and having nothing better to do in the interim, he decided to page through some of the materials he'd gathered at the library, starting first with what he was least familiar with. A cursory glance at the Weber and Greenberg work showed that they had "proved" that spores and bacteria and encysted organic materials could survive in "space-like" conditions for potentially millions of years. Interesting—in a quirky sort of way, Mitchell thought, though he did wonder about the value of such a study.

He took up the Hoyle and Wickramasinghe material, only to find that they were stumping for the idea that evolution was directed by the Earth's passage through space-borne spore clouds. Definitely a fringe idea, but Mitchell supposed one needed to know where the fringe was if one wanted to find out where the mainstream was headed. Maybe these two were just older scientists, proposing this concept in their dotage.

Mitchell picked up the copy of Arrhenius's *Worlds in the Making* and began leafing through that. Abruptly his eye caught on a word that, despite his brain-fogging exhaustion, made lots of things fall into place. Panspermia. Mitchell bit down on a fingernail as he read Arrhenius's description of spores lofting out of the atmospheres of life-bearing planets and drifting through the vastness of space to colonize other planets, infecting them with life.

Mitchell was tempted to drop the book like a tainted thing. He had always hated this "alternative" spores-from-outer-space explanation for the origin of life on Earth. It didn't explain anything about the deeper origins of life—just said, "Oh, life here came from somewhere else, and that life came from somewhere else, and before that from somewhere else." The whole idea came perilously close to an infinite regress, and was, at the very least, a hideous violation of the principle of Occam's razor.

He put Arrhenius's book quickly aside and, hoping to find something more rational, picked up the photocopied stack of the Francis Crick material and began to read. Soon he was lobe-deep in Crick's suggestion that these space spores were deliberately released by aliens in a direct attempt to colonize lifeless planets—

"Oh, for crying out loud!" Mitchell said, exasperated, tossing such back-door teleological nonsense as far away from him as he could manage, which at least landed it at the other side of the room.

His door buzzer sounded. Tiredly he got up and walked over to answer it. Lynda Tillman was there, looking as tired and overwrought as he felt. He invited her in. They made small talk for a while, but neither of them were really up for it. Preoccupied, he glanced out the windows at the lights of the city.

"Mitchell," Lynda said, from over near the counter by the kitchen nook, "this isn't over."

"It is for me," Mitchell said, moving slowly toward her.

"We both saw it!" Lynda insisted.

"There was no evidence," Mitchell said flatly, leaning on the counter. "We saw what we wanted to see."

"You didn't want to," Lynda said, her voice rising.

"That's just it," Mitchell said, practically pounding his palm against his forehead. "I wanted to believe. All this time I really just wanted to believe."

"Why is that such a crime?" Lynda asked, stepping deeply into his personal space.

"Because I threw away everything I've worked for!" Mitchell said, stepping back, gesturing too broadly and betraying more emotion than he would have liked. It was just that he was tired, so tired—of everything.

"Mitchell, we weren't drunk!" Lynda said, her voice rising and overcome with emotion, too. "You have to believe—"

"It wasn't real!" Mitchell said, grabbing Lynda by the shoulders, shouting at her. "Accept it! Your boy is gone! He ran away—and he ran away from you!"

"No!" Lynda said tearfully, shrugging out of his grip, her hands balling into loose fists. "I know Derek! There has to be more! There has to be more—"

Seeing the tearful woman before him, Mitchell felt horribly ashamed. He'd had no right to lash out at her that way—so personally.

"Lynda, I'm sorry," he said lamely, trying to reach out to her though she still pulled away. "I shouldn't have said that."

Lynda nodded—absently, tearfully—to herself, seemingly ready to leave. To his own surprise as much as hers, he found himself taking her by the wrists, then by the hands.

"Wait," he said, softly, then very close as he looked into her tear-streaked face. "I know what it's like to lose someone. To want that person back so hard it hurts. You don't deserve to be talked to like that, and I'm sorry."

Lynda knew the comfort he offered was heartfelt and real. She lifted her own hand to his face and kissed the hand holding it. As they came together in a mutually consoling embrace, Mitchell kissed her tenderly on the cheek. They stood there hugging and holding each other, until they moved to the couch. There she lay with her head on his shoulder until they both fell asleep in each other's arms, still fully clothed.

Morning sunlight awakened Mitchell. Finding himself arm-in-arm with Lynda on the couch, he was a bit disoriented for a moment. Realizing the situation, he sat up, Lynda's arm trailing off from around his waist.

"What's wrong?" Lynda asked.

"You're right," Mitchell said, standing up from the couch, making his way to a wicker armchair near the window and sitting down there. "I haven't gone on with my life. I haven't let go of her."

Lynda wondered again if Mitchell dreamed of his

late wife as if she were still alive. She knew she dreamed often of her son, going on about his life, very much alive. It was as if her conscious mind, her daylight mind, knew that Derek was dead, but her dreaming and unconscious mind refused to admit it.

"It's time you did, Mitchell," she said, also speaking to herself, and for herself.

"I know," Mitchell said from the wicker chair, looking at Lynda sitting up with her sleep-mussed hair, looking all the more attractive despite—or perhaps because of—that. "But Carrie's still real to me. I guess I really do believe in ghosts—because I've got one of my own. I'm sorry. I've still got some things to work out here."

Lynda understood what he was saying, all too clearly. She stood and headed for the table where she had left her sweater, though she couldn't now remember exactly when it was she'd taken it off.

"Are you going to be okay?" Mitchell asked, watching her, perhaps knowing too that he was saying much more in the subtext than in those surface words.

"Yeah," Lynda said, putting on her sweater and heading toward the door. "I'll bring you your money."

"I don't want your money," he said, standing up. "I . . . I won't take your money."

Standing by the door, she gave him a sad smile.

"Goodbye, Mitchell," she said, leaving through the door and closing it behind her. Absently, Mitchell moved toward the door, then stopped, walking back toward the window, flopping down in the wicker chair again two-thirds of the way there, thoughtful, trying to get things straight in his head.

The phone rang with its usual urgency. Mitchell got up slowly from the chair and went to answer it, standing by the window and looking out.

"Mitchell?" Jennifer's voice said. "Can you get down here right away?"

"Yeah," Mitchell said, watching Lynda get into her old gold-colored Buick in the street below. "Why?"

"I really think you need to see this," Jennifer said, sounding hurried and harried.

Mitchell felt a pang as he watched Lynda's car drive off.

"Okay," he said with a sigh, "I'm on my way." He hung up the phone, feeling very little enthusiasm for any more surprises.

When he arrived at Sheffield's complex of physics and chemistry buildings, Jennifer was in the exact opposite frame of mind. She was wired, hyped to near-bursting, mug of coffee in one hand, cigarette in the other.

"You were right," she said as they made their way down a corridor to her lab. "It is a meteorite."

"Yeah," he said foggily, "but what was Abrams doing with a meteorite in his house?"

"You tell me," Jennifer said as they turned a corner. "I'll bet you it wasn't the meteorite he was interested in, though. It's what was in the meteorite."

"What was that?" Mitchell asked.

"An enzyme," Jennifer said proudly.

"Enzyme?"

"That's the best word I can come up with for it," she said as they walked. "Not one that comes from Earth, though—unless we're willing to reinvent biochemistry."

"That's what Abrams was working with," Mitchell said, more pieces clicking together in his mind.

"Right," Jennifer said as they pushed through the door into her lab. They headed toward the large, glassed-in glove box. A stoppered Erlenmeyer flask, a greenish-yellow liquid covering its bottom to a depth of about a half inch, was clearly visible inside the glassed-in booth of the glove box.

"What am I looking at?" Mitchell asked.

"I was able to extract a small particle," Jennifer said, putting her hands in the gauntlets and picking up a pair of tongs, moving them to within a couple of inches of the stopper at the top of the flask. "Keep your eye on the Erlenmeyer."

Abruptly the rubber stopper on the flask lost its rigidity and, with a flowing leap of amoeboid motion, shot out a pseudopod that attached itself to the tip of the tongs.

"What the hell?" Mitchell asked, astounded.

"My words exactly," Jennifer said as they watched the animated rubbery thing feel and suck at the end of the tong, as if in search of food. Jennifer pulled away the tongs. The rubbery form wavered for a moment, then settled back into the mouth of the Erlenmeyer in its original, nobody-but-us-stoppers-here shape.

"I'd just placed the particle in the flask, heating it

in a weak carbonic acid solution," Jennifer said, "when I got called away for an hour. When I came back, it was like this."

"What is that, though?" Mitchell asked. "What happened to the rubber stopper?"

"It's still a rubber stopper," Jennifer said, almost embarrassed. "It just happens to be alive."

"Alive?" Mitchell asked, incredulous.

"In theory," Jennifer said with a nod. "Under high-powered microscopy, it appears to be a system capable of metabolizing, excreting, and breathing. It's obviously responsive to external stimuli, too."

"But how?" Mitchell asked, walking around the glove-box booth.

"Well, I've called it an enzyme," Jennifer said, "but it brings on a catalytic reaction unlike anything I've ever heard of. The way it organizes its environment, it's almost as if it functions like a cross between a protein and that nanotech stuff everybody talks about but nobody's really made happen yet."

"So your 'enzyme' reorganizes inanimate matter into a form of animate matter," Mitchell said, "and it's self-replicating."

"Yeah, that's about it," Jennifer said, pulling her hands out of the gauntlets. "The replication rate is astronomical. Lucky for us, it seems to have a problem with glass. The enzyme must have lain dormant in the meteorite. I think some combination of temperature, carbon, and water must have set off its alarm."

"Abrams set off its alarm too," Mitchell said. "And

its replication rate isn't the only thing about it that's astronomical."

"What do you mean?" Jennifer asked, picking up her mug of coffee. "And just exactly who was this Abrams guy, anyway?"

"He was a senior scientist working with Genedyne, a biotech firm that got closed down by the EPA," Mitchell said. "That meteorite came from a very private lab, in the house he apparently abandoned."

"How did he find it, though?" Jennifer asked. "And what did he want with the stuff inside it?

Mitchell thought hard before he spoke.

"Have you ever heard of panspermia?"

"Pan-what?" Jennifer asked.

"Panspermia," Mitchell repeated.

"Sounds like a guy thing," Jennifer said, giving him a wry look.

"In some ways, I suppose it is," Mitchell said, seriously. "Almost all the scientists who have advocated it are male. Svante Arrhenius came up with it in 1908. Basically it's the idea that organic material—spores, encysted proteins, your 'enzyme'—can be lofted out of a planet's biosphere, drift across deep space, and land on the surface of another planet, still viable. In its extreme form, panspermia means that life on Earth began when one of these little seeds of life landed here, after traveling who knows how far through outer space."

"Little organic sperm, fertilizing a rock-planet ovum?" Jennifer asked, then nodded and smiled. "A guy thing, all right."

Mitchell glanced down at the floor, smiling himself, but only for a moment.

"Maybe, but Abrams seems to have been a guy who was very much into this sort of thing. He was a believer in panspermia—that's why he was collecting meteorites, especially carbonaceous chondrites. The idea of panspermia itself may have survived only in fringe science and science fiction circles, but Abrams must have thought it had some merit. Judging by what he found, he seems to have been right."

Jennifer sat down on a swiveling lab chair.

"But what was he after, in trying to trigger it?" she asked.

Mitchell leaned up against a counter, crossing his arms.

"Think about it. This stuff can impart animation to inanimate matter. If he activated it, then learned how to 'program' it, he could steal a march on everybody—the biotechnicians, the nanotechnologists, all the high-stakes players. What the atomic bomb was to physics, this would be to the biological sciences. The EPA must have gotten wind of what Genedyne was doing, messing with alien organics, so they shut them down. Abrams, though, was hooked. He must have kept working on the project at home, where it got away from him."

"What do you mean?" Jennifer asked, coming to her feet and looking genuinely shocked.

"I mean part of the Abrams house is just like that rubber stopper," Mitchell said quietly. "It's been infected by that alien 'enzyme.'"

"Are you sure?"

Mitchell nodded.

"God, if this stuff is out in the real world," Jennifer said, a shiver running through her despite herself, "there's no reason it couldn't keep spreading as long as it had enough to eat."

"We have to find some way to neutralize it," Mitchell said resolutely.

For the next several hours, the two of them spent their time methodically thinking up ways to kill the enzyme-possessed stopper. Exposing it to heat or cold, however, merely made it demonstrate its ability to move evasively or go into its stopper-shaped "rest state." Depriving it of oxygen or pumping the glovebox full of carbon monoxide harmed the "enzyme" not in the least. The stopper began to seem disturbingly unstoppable.

"Two cc's chlorobenzene," Jennifer said, her gauntleted hands moving a syringe loaded with that amount in the direction of the not-so-innocent rubber stopper in the Erlenmeyer. "No way it can swallow this."

The stopper flung out a pseudopod like a black frog's tongue snagging a fly, wrapping firmly around the business end of the hypodermic. Jennifer pumped down the plunger of the hypodermic, injecting the chlorobenzene into the stopper's pseudopod, then moved the hypodermic out of the stopper's striking range. The stopper bubbled and bulged, alive as ever or maybe more so, then at last settled back down into its stopper-shaped resting form.

Jennifer sighed.

"Not only is it alive," she said, "but it's determined to stay that way."

Mitchell nodded, leaning against the large glove box, thoughtful.

"If it's alive," he said with determination, "it can die."

They continued for several more hours, throwing a good percentage of the entire chemistry department stockroom at the stopper, but nothing stopped it. Acids, alkalis, heavy metals, organics, sulfates, sulfites, nitrates, nitrites, poisons of a dozen different stripes—all were injected, becoming simply grist for the unstoppable stopper's mill, taken in as food or ignored and excreted.

As their final witches' brew failed, Mitchell and Jennifer at last stepped dejectedly away from the glassed-in booth of the glove box and paused to regroup and rethink.

"That's everything but the kitchen sink," Jennifer said, "and if we had one I'd try that too."

Mitchell, leaning against a countertop, ran his hands over his face and shook his head.

"There's got to be something it can't swallow," he said, gesturing with a lecturer's finger for emphasis.

"Maybe there isn't," Jennifer said in despair.

"No, whatever was in the Abrams house didn't get me, or Lynda, or Luther," Mitchell said, thinking it through. "There's got to be some reason—some reason we didn't get killed."

As Jennifer watched, Mitchell stood up and walked to the phone.

"What are you doing?" she asked.

"I'm going to make a fool of myself with the police for the second time in as many days," Mitchell said, punching in Sergeant Roth's number. As briefly and quickly as he could, Mitchell tried to explain to Roth what he and Jennifer had learned and to plead with Roth to get his men out of that house.

"Now let me get this straight," Roth said from his desk in the nearly deserted police station. "The house isn't haunted?"

"It doesn't make any difference what it is—" Mitchell said over the phone, his voice creaky with frustration.

"Then why should I get my men out?" Roth stubbornly wanted to know.

"Because something Abrams was working on has infected a portion of the house," Mitchell said, trying to explain as simply as possible, "and that is dangerous to people—"

"Mitchell, you were better off with your ghost story," Roth said, incredulously.

"Look, I don't care whether you believe me or not," Mitchell said, growing angry at the man on the other end of the line. "Just let me talk to Luther—"

"Luther Dobson is back on the street," Roth said flatly.

"On the street?"

"That's right," Roth said. "We didn't have enough evidence to hold him. If my men dig up something, we'll get him back. It's not like we don't know exactly where he goes. He's a transient with a limited range. I don't think he's been out of the county in twenty years. He's probably getting drunk as we speak."

Like a blue spike right between the eyes, a revelation hit Mitchell hard.

"Was Luther drunk when you found him?" he asked.

"Are you kidding?" Roth said. "Luther's been drunk since the day he was born."

Forgetting any sense of courtesy, Mitchell abruptly hung up the phone on Roth.

"Ethanol," Mitchell said to Jennifer. "Ethyl alcohol. It's worth a shot."

~~~~~~~~~~

Lynda Tillman had returned home from her visit with Mitchell feeling disappointed. Everything had concluded in such a dead-end manner that she began drinking early. That was how she spent the afternoon at home in Bellingham: watching brain-dead daytime TV, drinking scotch, and feeling quite honestly sorry for herself.

By evening, she sat slumped on her living room couch, surrounded by photos of Derek, and of herself and Derek together. Fighting back tears, she picked up a bottle of Seagram's, unscrewed it, and tried to take a drink—only to find that the bottle was empty. That was the last liquor in the house. Frustrated, she tossed the bottle aside, then looked a long while at the phone, thinking of the police.

At the Abrams place, though, the Bellingham

police had been very busy already. A pair of patrol cars and a coroner's Jeep stood parked out front. Officer Gould and his team had strung yellow POLICE LINE DO NOT CROSS tape through the fences around the Abrams property during the morning. With the coroner in tow, they had searched all the rooms in the house. Finding nothing, they had headed toward the basement.

Late in the afternoon, the officers decided they would begin digging in search of human remains there, as soon as they could run power and lights into the place. By the time the Abrams place stood framed in sunset light, the police had a portable generator up and running nearby. Electrical cables snaked through the front door and into the house. As soon as they finished stringing lights along the basement ceiling, the officers began digging with shovels into the dirt of the unfloored section of the basement.

One of Gould's men, Mike Leitner, soon unearthed what looked like the end of a bone. He called to the coroner, silver-haired Warren Watkins, who began dusting away debris from the bone with a broad paintbrush. Gould phoned the information in to Roth at headquarters.

No sooner had Roth gotten off the phone with Gould, though, than his office phone rang again.

"Roth here."

"This is Lynda Tillman," said the voice on the other end of the line. "Have you found anything?"

"No, we haven't found anything yet, Mrs. Tillman," Roth said, not quite truthfully.

"I'm going to go over to the house," Lynda Tillman said, determination in her voice.

"That's a very bad idea, Ms. Tillman," Roth said, very much wanting to discourage her. "When a person comes out of the ground—"

"I don't care," Lynda said. "I should be there if they find Derek."

Before he could say anything more, Lynda Tillman hung up. Great, just great, Roth thought. He had been hoping for a quiet evening, but now he'd have to go out to the Abrams place and either stop the woman from doing what she planned, or comfort her once she'd done it. He had to finish up this report here first, but once he was done he'd head out to the crime scene just as quickly as he could.

Roth shook his head. Some days it just didn't pay to be a cop.

~~~~~~~~~~

"Okay," Jennifer said, screwing the cap back onto a bottle labeled "Ethyl Alcohol." "Why alcohol?"

"Lynda, Luther, and I all had one thing in common," Mitchell said, his hands deep in the glove-box gauntlets, holding an ethanol-loaded syringe in his gloved hands.

"What?" Jennifer asked from behind him.

"We'd all been drinking."

Mitchell brought the alcohol-filled syringe up within range of the stopper. It shot out its black frog's tongue of pseudopod.

"To our success," Mitchell said in mock-toast as he

began pushing on the hypo's plunger. He squinted with concentration as he pumped the last of the syringe's alcohol into the amoeboid rubber stopper. The stopper convulsed inward, wriggled and quivered and dribbled back down inside the Erlenmeyer, as if trying to escape. Formless, it plopped down inside the bottom of the flask, emitting a brownish smoke, the stopper discoloring to a whitish-brown goop, then a yellowish slime.

"You may be alien," Mitchell said triumphantly, "but you can't hold your liquor."

At his shoulder, Jennifer laughed. Mitchell turned to her.

"I need all the alcohol you've got," Mitchell said, "and a large portable pump sprayer—at least five gallon capacity."

With Jennifer's help, it took him only moments to gather the necessary materials and dash off to his Jeep. Soon he was careening down the highway at speeds in violation of city, county, state, national, and international limits—emptying bottles of pure ethyl alcohol into the sprayer's tank as he drove. If the police pulled him over, they'd have an "open container" bust to tell their grandkids about, and he wasn't even drinking!

~~~~~~~~~~

In the basement of the Abrams place, Gould and Leitner sweated away at their digging. Coroner Watkins came trotting down the basement stairs, a can of soda pop in each hand, going first to Leitner, then to Gould.

"Thanks, Warren," Leitner said.

"Thanks," Gould panted when Watkins gave him the can of pop. A beer would have been more satisfying, but he was on duty. Soda pop would have to do. Warren had gone back over to talk to Mike. Gould turned away, thinking about digging in a different direction. He chugged down the pop, set it aside, and wiped his brow. He was just about to start digging once more when the whole building began to shake.

"What was that?" Gould called above the rumbling din—and another sound, like someone's screaming, abruptly cut off. He turned around. Officer Leitner and Coroner Watkins were nowhere to be seen. Gould walked toward where he'd last seen the two of them.

"Mike?" he called. "Warren?"

The house began to shudder loudly once more.

"I'm getting the hell out of here," Gould said, flinging down his shovel and racing toward the basement stairs. He flew up them without thinking. In a moment he had reached the top of the stairs and was pounding through the foyer, but he discovered that the front door was so jammed that it might as well have been locked. Furiously but futilely he tugged at the door. The moaning and shuddering of the house grew still louder and stronger.

Above his head, Gould heard a sudden creaking so loud that for a moment it drowned out everything else. When he looked up, he saw that the chandelier a few feet above his head was descending toward him rapidly, opening hungrily, like a chromium flower of terrifying beauty.

"NOOOOO—" Gould screamed as the chandelier flower wrapped its metal tendrils around his head and shoulders. Lifting his body swiftly off the floor, it pulled his kicking and screaming form upward toward the ceiling so forcefully that one of Gould's shoes was left behind on the foyer floor, while its owner went against his will to find out himself where Leitner and Watkins had so abruptly disappeared to.

Despite all her brave talk to Roth on the phone, it took Lynda considerably more than an hour to summon up the courage to get in her car and drive out to the Abrams place for what might very well be the exhumation of her son's body. Even once she got out to her car, she sat behind the wheel a full fifteen minutes before she turned on the ignition. She drove out of town at a snail's pace.

Roth was similarly delayed. The report he had been working on had some major rough spots to finesse. He'd also heard nothing more from the forensic dig out at the crime scene. Presuming that no news was good news, he felt justified in taking the extra time on the report. If Ms. Tillman was out there waiting in the cold and damp of the night, it would serve her right for her bull-headedness.

Mitchell, on the other hand, was driving like a madman. The fates were with him, though. He'd covered far more distance in far less time than either Lynda or Roth, without being pulled over by the police. His only concern now was that he get to the Abrams place and destroy Abrams's horrible legacy before it killed anyone else—or spread irreversibly into the fabric of the environment itself. The empty ethyl alcohol bottles clanked and the capped tank sprayer sloshed heavily as Mitchell took the off-ramp into Bellingham a little too fast. Almost there, he thought, almost there.

Lynda still got there first, though. In her old gold Buick she pulled up beside the empty patrol cars and behind the coroner's vehicle in front of the Abrams place. Still far from eager to face what she might encounter, she sat in her car for some time, staring toward the house. Might as well get it over with, she thought at last, opening the car door and stepping out, looking up toward the darkened house.

As she walked up the hill toward the front door, she was surprised to see no lights. She would have thought the place would be lit up like a Christmas tree, with the police working there. Maybe they only had their lights going in the basement, she thought as she pushed open the front door.

As she entered the foyer, the chandelier creaked lightly overhead. Her foot brushed against something. Looking down, she saw a man's shoe, black.

"Is anybody here?" she called into the darkness and silence of the abandoned house. She walked deeper into the foyer, then into the hallway that led from it. In the shaft of moonlight shining in through the back window, Lynda saw a shirtless figure in silhouette.

Derek!

"Oh my god," Lynda said, voice quavering with

emotion, torn between unbelievable hope and undeniable fear.

"It's me, Mom," said the figure with Derek's voice—or Derek's voice and something more, that resonant, reverberant voice that she had once heard coming from everywhere at once. She didn't want to hear it now. She just wanted to hear Derek, only Derek. She moved slowly toward him, then hesitated.

"Don't be afraid, Mom," Derek said. "There's no need to be afraid."

Derek's voice, with that other resonance she did not want to hear, was soothing, hypnotic. Lynda drew closer to the figure of her son, unearthly pale in the silver moonlight.

"It's okay here," Derek said as Lynda came closer and stood before him. "It's really okay."

As she looked into Derek's eyes, tears began to well up in Lynda's own.

"It's warm," Derek said, reaching out a hand and stroking the wall lightly. "Peaceful."

Under Derek's touch the wall seemed to ripple like water, or like the liquid muscles of a purring cat. If she saw it, Lynda put it out of her mind.

"Derek," she said, coming to him, embracing him with a mother's love, wrapping her sweatered arms about his pale naked torso in the pale moonlight. "I knew you'd come back to me," she said tearfully, "I knew it—"

Lynda, wrapped in the arms of her "son," barely noticed that he was edging her, drawing her, slowly toward the wall he had caressed earlier.

Behind them, Mitchell banged open the front door, lugging the heavy pump-sprayer. Seeing the darkened house, he had run up the hill as fast as his legs could carry him. Even so, it had seemed to take an eternity to get through the fence, the weed-choked yard, up the front steps. What Mitchell saw now—Lynda in the arms of a teenaged boy, "Derek" staring toward Mitchell over his mother's shoulder with a slyly malevolent expression—made the scientist fear he had arrived too late.

"Get away from him!" Mitchell shouted.

Lynda moved back from "Derek."

"Lynda, that's not Derek!" Mitchell said, readying the sprayer. "It's the house—mimicking your son!"

"No-oo—" Lynda screamed as "Derek" betrayed her, grabbing her arm and, with superhuman strength, pulling her into the wall.

Mitchell ran forward, but the floorboards suddenly turned to animate quicksand beneath his feet, tripping him and catching him up. He fell to the floor, trapped.

Lynda and "Derek" popped back out of the wall. Lynda knew now that Derek's voice had been the siren song of Death, and that on the other side of that wall lay an oblivion more permanent than ever came out of a liquor bottle. Although her will to live was stronger than she had ever dreamed, she could not last long against the unbelievable devouring strength of the house.

Mitchell, seeing Lynda and "Derek" in the hall again for at least a moment, sprayed them and the wall with as much alcohol as he could. Enraged, "Derek" and the house pulled Lynda back farther into the wall. The quicksand-soft floor surged up to Mitchell's waist. With a roar of his own, Mitchell took the nozzle end of the sprayer and plunged it into the flesh-rippling floor like a harpoon. As the hungry vortex of the house reached up Mitchell's torso toward his shoulders and head, Mitchell drew the tank of the sprayer down with him, switched open and draining into the maw of the house as it devoured him. The last thing he saw was the quivering ceiling, the carpeted floor sloshing over him like a paisley wave, then everything going a sickly green, then dark. Around him sounded innumerable heartbeats, innumerable screams.

Outside, Sergeant Roth pulled up with two more officers. He had had no reports from his officers on scene or from the coroner for too long. He didn't know what to expect, but it certainly wasn't anything like what he saw when he and his officers clambered out of the car.

Lights flashed erratically from the house and windows shattered, as if from explosions. In an instant, though, it was clear that what was happening was not an explosion but an implosion. With an enormous roar and clatter the entire edifice of the Abrams house was settling in on itself, collapsing inward and downward. The whole huge old Queen Anne mansion began slumping down like swiftly melting candlewax, liquefying and disintegrating. The clatter of collapse, the flashes and smoke, for all their violence, were not nearly so horrid as the realization that the once seemingly-solid structure was degenerating into a flood of ghastly, stinking ooze that was swamping the grounds where the home had once stood.

"Good God," Roth said, staring in amazement at

the yellow-brown swampy muck dribbling down the hill from where the house had once stood.

If Roth was amazed by what he was seeing, Mitchell was far more amazed by what he was experiencing. He was inundated by a flashing tidal wave of other people's memories: Gould and Leitner and Watkins, Nadia and Derek and Abrams himself, and several more he could not identify. Then he felt the memory that encompassed all of those, a memory of shock and heat, and beyond that an interminable passage through the cold night that lies between the stars.

Was this a near-death experience? Mitchell wondered. Was he in fact already dead? If he were dying, though, shouldn't the life passing in front of his eyes be his own?

As the passage between the stars continued and led him from world to world, he realized that the life passing dreamlike in front of him was definitely someone—or something—else's. The alien "enzyme," he now knew, was a great deal more than that. It was an organic information technology of such rich complexity that it made DNA look like a denatured and degraded descendant.

In a vast collective consciousness, it remembered everywhere it had ever been, and everything it remembered Mitchell now experienced: the life it had given birth to on many planets, the life destroyed and supplanted on not a few more, its own birthworld, its creation by the long-lived, tentacled sapients of the littoral zones of its watery birth planet, bent not only on extending their own consciousnesses as far as possible, but also on lifting into higher consciousness all living things, even the whole universe itself so that, in the Eschaton Moment of perfect universal consciousness, the old universe might pass away and a new and transcendent one take its place.

Something had gone wrong, though. The substance the ancient masters had intended to set free into the universe so that it might infect non-life with life—the organic information technology they had hoped would direct that new life on the long road toward higher consciousness and sentience—the "enzyme" that ought to have been hailed as something godlike—soon enough proved prone to becoming not a god but a toxic pollutant, a great plague of conformity supplanting diversity, wherever found, with its own program and programming.

Fearing that their creation might supplant or destroy highly evolved life and mind that had arisen independently elsewhere in the universe, yet hoping still to salvage the magnificence of what they had made and the greatness of its mission, the creators reengineered their problem-child as much as they could. The organic information technology would become activated only by conditions prevailing in parabiotic situations—those under which life could take hold but had not yet done so. Over millennia in activated form, the "enzyme" would also mutate and degrade into safer, less invasive forms of information storage.

As a final added safeguard, the creators had restructured the "enzyme" so that, should it come into contact with a technological society advanced enough to trigger its properties, the organic technology would grow relatively slowly in biotic conditions, hopefully slowly enough for that society to eradicate it by exploiting the failsafe vulnerability the tentacled creators had engineered into it: namely, a fatal sensitivity to ethyl alcohol.

Having done all that, the creators could restrain their problem-child no longer. It spread through the universe, on a journey so long that time and eternity became indistinguishable.

As the dreamlike memories faded, part of Mitchell's mind realized that, in his own warped way, Luther had been right: consciousnesses within consciousnesses, a troubled and troubling god hungry after millennia in the desert of space. The poor, the street people, really do enter the kingdom of God first, Mitchell thought distantly. Or at least they are the first to experience the future.

Mitchell abruptly returned to ordinary consciousness, webbed with slime, gagging and gasping for breath, with only one thought on his mind.

"Lynda!" he called out as he got to his hands and knees, then shakily to his feet. He stumbled about, covered with muck. The house had turned to a fetid swamp, steaming and smoking, even burning like flaring marsh gas in one corner. Strewn about the swampy grounds and muck-flooded basement were those parts—usually metal—which the alien substance had not converted into its own, as well as the skeletal remains of people and animals, including forms only half digested because more recently ingested.

"Oh my god," he mumbled as he staggered about

the steaming charnel-house ruins, fearing that every skeleton or half-consumed corpse might be the remains of the woman that he now realized he loved. "Oh my god."

That was all he could say: the mindless mantra of some primal faith. All he could say when he spotted a woman coated in slime and muck like himself, face up in the muck, unmoving: Lynda. All he could say as he came to her, lifted her, cradled her, as she coughed and came gasping back to life, back to her life, and back to his.

From the edge of the rise, Sergeant Roth and his officers watched, bewildered bystanders in the immediate aftermath of a local apocalypse, staring without understanding at what catastrophe had revealed.

~~~~~~~~~~

Into cloudy overcast skies a few hours later, the sun rose and the birds called, as on any other morning. At the increasingly crowded crime scene, Roth took notes. He had been taking notes for the last several hours—statements from Leviticus Mitchell and Lynda Tillman, descriptions of the crime scene, descriptions of what he himself had seen. What a long, strange night it had been.

He looked around at the other authorities who had arrived on site: county sheriff's people, state troopers, a Hazardous Materials team. Officials from Washington State and Federal EPA were due in, early this morning. He wouldn't be surprised if the military and intelligence people dropped by before this was all over. The only thing that was going to be more of a mess than the sludge that had been the Abrams place, he thought, was the tangle of reports and red tape yet to come.

Lynda Tillman was sitting over on the hood of Mitchell's truck, gazing up at where the house used to be. Mitchell was coming down from the hilltop ruins. He seemed to have taken enough "samples," for now. Both of them were wrapped in civil defense-issue blankets and looked like survivors of some unnamable disaster. That was appropriate, at least, Roth thought.

"No," Roth said, noticing a state trooper about to toss away a torn bit of shoe leather. "Here. That's evidence."

Mitchell came around the corner of his Jeep, catching Lynda's glance, looking into her eyes.

"Shall we go?" he asked.

"Do you think it's really over?" Lynda wondered.

"I don't know," he said, subdued. "We may never know."

"I guess it's just a matter of faith," Lynda said evenly.

"Just a matter of faith," Mitchell said, nodding.

He helped her down from the hood of the Jeep. Putting his arm around her, he led her around to the passenger-side door and opened it for her, then walked around to the driver's side.

As he started the Jeep and pulled around, he wanted to ask Lynda if she too had undergone that strange time, like a near-death or out-of-body experience, in which all the hungry god's dying memories had passed before the mind's eye, epochs passing in an instant. Mitchell glanced at her and saw that she was tired. Such questions could wait. They would have time. He knew that, now.

It was true, he thought as they drove away. Life did go on, like everybody always told him after he lost Carrie, like everybody always tells anyone who has experienced that everyday end of the world, the unexpected loss of a loved one. What they never told you, though, was that it never went on the same.

Mitchell and Lynda would get on with their lives, but not the same. Maybe, just maybe, getting on with a life together would prove to be better than getting on alone.

~~~~~~~~~~

HOWARD HENDRIX has been selling science fiction and horror stories for ten years. He has sold two novels to Berkley/Ace (watch for Lightpaths *in 1997 and* Standing Wave *in 1998). His stories have appeared in* Amazing Stories, Isaac Asimov's Science Fiction Magazine, Full Spectrum, *and* Writers of the Future, *among many other places. He won a Writers of the Future First Place Award in 1986 and a Theodore Sturgeon Award in 1994.*

Dr. Hendrix (Ph.D. in English Literature, 1987) is the head of the School of Arts and Sciences at California State University at Fresno, though he is currently on sabbatical while finishing Standing Wave.

"I chose this episode," he told us, "because it reminded me of two of my favorite dark tales: Edgar Allan Poe's 'The Fall of the House of Usher' and H. P. Lovecraft's 'The Colour out of Space,' both of which hammered new dents in my malleable young mind before I was old enough to know better." Think about it—Hendrix could have been reading "Great Books" instead, and our genre would be the poorer for it.

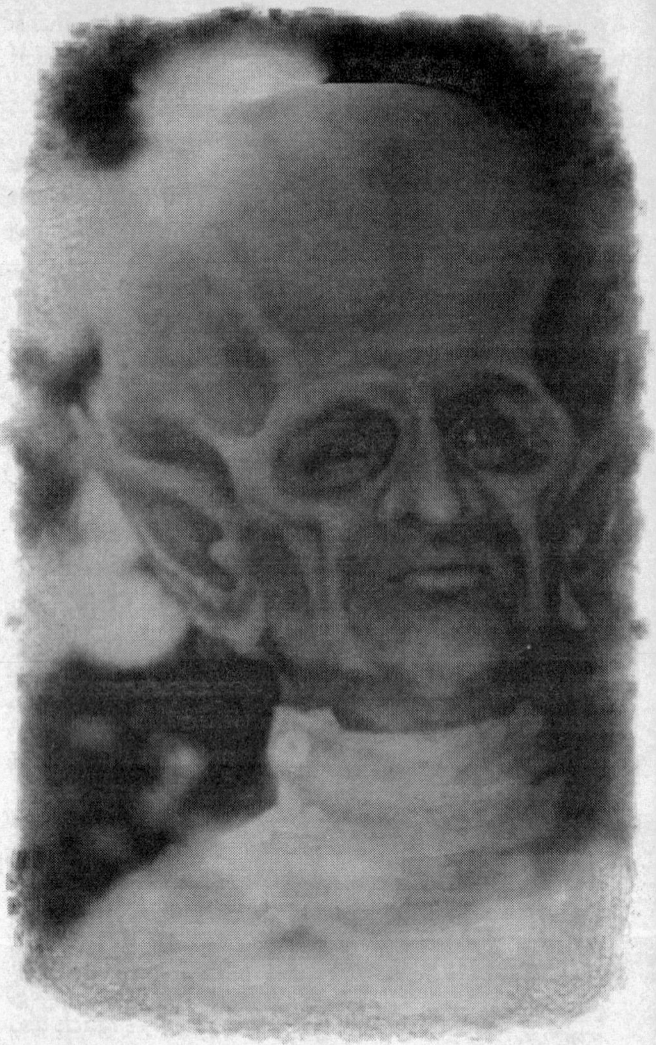

No story haunts the human imagination like that of Frankenstein, the obsessed scientist who created a monster he could not control. In "The Sixth Finger," a popular episode from the 1960s, screenwriter Ellis St. Joseph took Mary Shelley's concept one step further: suppose a scientist started with a human being as his original subject?

Set in the mining communities of Wales, "The Sixth Finger" is a memorable and disturbing thought-experiment about what might happen to an ordinary man who was suddenly advanced through thousands of years of evolution . . . and what might happen to the ordinary woman who loved him.

The Sixth Finger

Adaptation by John M. Ford
Original Screenplay by Ellis St. Joseph

THE TOWN had a name, though no one used it much. The English said it was a long Welsh name, full of improper letters and impossible to spell. To the people who lived there, well, it was just the town; one might name other towns, Aberteifi or Llandrinod Wells, but this was the place one lived and dwelt and died, no forgetting what it was.

The town sat in a narrow part of the Rhondda Valley, on three modest coal seams; it might have vanished long ago but for them. Now, after years and years of mining, the jumble of frame houses was shadowed by great shapeless piles of black slag, reaching halfway up the slope in places. The mine—which had a name, too, but again, there was no other—had grown bigger than the town itself, spreading out its fences and barren gravel lots and rusty metal sheds like a growth of harsh weed taking over a garden, the high iron gallows of the hoist frames blossoming stark above.

Still, the mine made work, and without work how should men have their bread?

Every morning saving Sundays, Cathy Evans tucked a dozen loaves of her sister Gert's warm white bread into her basket, covered them neatly with a white linen, and began the long walk around town to deliver them. First four loaves went to the house of Mr. Caradoc, who owned the coal mine that was the town's whole livelihood, one to the mine manager's, one to the foreman's, then a loaf to the banker, and Jones the Fixit-man, and so up the one main street; and then the last loaf along the side road up the steep valley wall, to the Ives house, where the Englishman was living.

Then, when she was done, she could pause for a few minutes up on the slope, a little above the town and the smoke. On a breezy day, like this one, the Ives house was clear above the gray. Gwilym Griffiths had shown her hidden paths here, where they could climb into the clean air, see bits and patches of the Rhondda Vale as it must have been when the coal was all still hidden, a hundred years or more ago.

But she and Gwilym had done that long ago, when they were still both young enough that to go on such a hike was merely childish mischief. She was eighteen, now, and Gwilym a terribly grown-up twenty-five, and it would no longer do.

She rearranged her woolen shawl over her straight, golden hair. The shawl had once been a pretty autumn russet, but three years of coalsmoke and dust had turned it a sorry brown. The linen covering the bread in her basket was clean, though; Cathy washed it, pounding and scrubbing it, twice a week, and folded the cloths in a tight cupboard where mine dust could not reach them. Gert the Bread insisted on that. Gert always insisted on proper work from other people.

The Ives house had two floors and a fine slate chimney. Mr. Ives had been part owner of the mine, with Mr. Caradoc, until the black lung took him. Everyone in town thought he was rich, but he wasn't after all, and Mrs. Ives had lived on this and that until the Englishman came to rent the place.

As Cathy got near the door, she heard a high, almost whistling sound. It seemed to shake her bones. For a horrible instant she thought it was the alarm whistle from the mine, but then it stopped. A crow in a tree began screeching in protest, and Cathy glared at it. Sometimes the crows would snatch her fresh bread. Gert never believed that, always called Cathy a liar who had eaten the loaf herself, demanded that she pay for it—and since Cathy never had a penny of her own, launder an extra week's linens to make up. Cathy thought her hands must turn into crow's claws, just as the miners' hands went black forever.

She knocked at the door. She looked at her hand; it still seemed pretty enough. There was no answer. She knocked again.

"Mrs. Ives!" she called. "Mrs. Ives!"

Still no answer. She tried the door, which opened. Beyond it was a hall, lit only by the light through the door, unswept for what must have been weeks. She took a cautious step inside.

The whining sound started again. It was coming from a room at the side of the hall, a closed door with light showing under its crooked jamb.

If she took the loaf of bread back down the valley side, Gert would say she had never delivered it. If she left it without collecting the money, Gert would—no, she simply had to find someone and collect. She went through the door. She gasped.

She was in what must have been a grand front parlor. There was carved wooden trim in the corners, and a fine fireplace. But the room was entirely full of machinery: racks of glass tubes, coils of wire, metal cases with small glowing lights and knobs. Desks and filing cabinets took up most of the remaining space. It was like Jones's tinker shop in town, gone all mad. Blackboards and cork boards were pinned all over the walls, blocking off most of the light from the windows; cold tube lights made up the difference.

A man in a dingy white smock was crouched over one of the cabinets. He turned suddenly. He was tall and pale, and his hair was tangled; he wore glasses, and his face was set hard. He turned a big switch, and the sound died away. "What're you doing here?"

"I'm Cathy Evans. . . . I brung yer fresh bread. Mrs. Ives needs t'pay me."

"That woman's never about when she's wanted! Impossible to get proper help around here. I can't even find an assistant—" The man turned, looked down at his hand, which was gripping a pair of fine-nosed pliers. He seemed puzzled by them, then put them down. "Fresh bread, you say? Give it here!"

Cathy turned back the white linen and took out the last of Gert's warm loaves. The man snatched it from her and tore into it, his fingers cracking the hard crust. Cathy held out her hand and said, "One shilling and tuppence, please."

Still eating with his left hand, the man dug into his pocket with the other. He dumped a handful of coins on a table and picked up a few. As he held them out, he paused, and his face softened. "I'm sorry, miss. Not always so rude. I haven't stopped to eat this morning, and I worked through the night—"

"That's all right, sir," Cathy said. She looked around at the strange, fantastical room. "What kind of work is it ye do here?"

"I'm a geneticist. Professor of genetics. . . . My name's Mathers. And you're Cathy? You make the bread?"

"Cathy Evans, sir. Gert the Bread is my older sister."

"Ah. I'm afraid I don't get into town much . . . . Look, have you any more bread?"

"That was the last, sir. . . . I can bring you more, if you can wait."

Mathers gave a dry laugh. "Wait. Yes, I can wait. But hurry. I can never wait too long for anything." And he turned back to his machines.

Cathy bowed and started for the door. Then she stopped. "Genetics?"

"Genetics," Mathers said.

"And you're a professor of them?"

"Indeed. When I am not also a physicist, a biochemist, a mathematician, a biologist—" He picked up the pliers again. "And a mechanical engineer. Though if pressed, my specialty is evolutionary dynamics."

Cathy's mouth opened. She said, "E-vo-lu-tion's only a . . . a theory."

"Gravity's only a theory," Mathers said amiably, "but I wouldn't walk off any roofs if I were you."

Suddenly a monkey swung into the room from somewhere in the rear. He was chattering furiously, and jumped up on a desk near Mathers, holding out his paws.

After a startled moment, Cathy found herself delighted. She had never seen a live monkey before, certainly never supposed they could be housepets.

Mathers said, "You're hungry, too, eh, Darwin? We've put in a hard night! Here." He handed the monkey the last bit of bread. The animal took it, nodded, and ate it with considerably better manners than Mathers had used.

"Oh! What a creature! Have you taught him any tricks?"

"Oh . . . more than tricks. Darwin earns his keep." Mathers picked up a stack of papers from the desk, and held them out to the monkey. "File these notes, Darwin. Right cabinet, under Molecular Genetics."

To Cathy's astonishment, the monkey swung to the side of the room, and put the papers into a file folder. Then he looked among the drawers, peering at the little labels, opened one, and put the folder neatly in place, just like a secretary at the bank.

She said, "However did he become so smart?"

Mathers tilted his head. "I made him that way."

"Never . . ."

Mathers said seriously, "I am not playing with you. Darwin is a chimpanzee, a highly intelligent species to begin with. I have taken him somewhat farther."

Cathy struggled to imagine it. Professors were teachers, she knew, like at university, but genetics— "Can you do that with people, too? Teach them to be smart?"

"It takes a little more than teaching," Mathers said. He gestured at the machines in the room, at a big metal box in the corner with a glass window in its front. Then he let his arm drop, tiredly. "And yes, my dear, I very much hope to do it with people. Why do you wonder?"

"I'd like to be smart." She felt her heart tighten. "There's someone I'd like to be smart for."

Mathers sat on a stool and pressed his hands together. There was a new brightness in his face. "Who are your parents?"

"They're dead, sir. There's only me, and Gert, and Gert doesn't—Could you make me half-way smart?"

Mathers fidgeted a bit. Then, very firmly, he said, "We could try. I'll need a sample of your blood."

"Blood?"

"Just a few ccs—just a little. There'll be a needle, but I promise it won't hurt much." He smiled. "Isn't that what doctors always say?" He went to a wall cabinet.

"So you're a doctor, too, then?"

"Oh," Mathers said absently, "yes, that too." He took a paper envelope from the cabinet, opened it and produced a hypodermic syringe.

Darwin the chimp chattered at the sight of the needle, and covered his eyes with his paws.

"Oh, come now, Darwin, this isn't even for you. Be brave. Are we not men?" Mathers took cotton and alcohol from the cabinet, said gently, "Roll up your sleeve, Cathy, and make a good tight fist."

She squeaked a little as the needle stuck her, but Mathers had told the truth: it did not really hurt. And he clearly had no wish to hurt her. That made a great difference.

~~~~~~~~~~~~~~~

Gert Evans was angry, not that there was anything unusual about that. She sat before the cashbox in the tiny front of the bakery, between yesterday's bread loaves (twopenny discount) and a glass-covered cake that had been old when Elizabeth took the throne, counting a handful of coins for at least the fifth time.

"Twelve and one, and two, and three," she said. "You went out with a round dozen loaves, at a shilling-tuppence each; that ought make fourteen bob, oughtn't it? Well, girl, oughtn't it?"

Cathy was leaning against the end of the counter, looking in the direction of the hills, of the Ives house. She had already been scolded once for coming back late; she was past feeling this, and far away. She held her arm, with the Professor's needle mark secret beneath her sleeve. "I s'pose it ought, Gert."

"Then where's the one and nine ye're short? Stol'n it, haven't you?"

"No, Gert."

"Them *boys* may think you Miss Innocent," Gert exploded, "but not I! Not your sister, who you think no better of than t'thieve from!" She threw the coins into the box, slammed its lid, and came waddling around the counter. Her baggy eyes were squeezed narrow, and she was wiping her hands eagerly on her dingy apron. She seized Cathy's shoulders and shook her hard. "You'll give it to me now, or—"

"Gert, I ha'n't *got* it. The Professor—"

"The what?"

"The Englishman. Up the hill. He was all busy, he must have given me the wrong—"

"Enough lyin'! I'll teach you to count, my girl, if I have to knock it into you!"

Cathy shoved Gert away with both hands, took three quick steps back. "I'll go back there, right now, and see he gives me the right change, Gert. Anyway, he wants another."

Gert didn't seem to hear. She came on, her fingers in claws and her face clouded with fury.

The door swung open, giving its rusty bell a dull jangle. Gert stopped still; she never struck Cathy with customers in the shop.

Two men stamped dirt from their pit boots and came in. They were both black with coal dust, their faces darkened, their hair thick with it; they had an ancient look, though Wilt Morgan was barely twenty and Gwilym Griffiths was twenty-five.

"'Ere, Miss Witch," Wilt said cheerfully, "leave that helpless child be!"

"Child, aye," Gert said. "Not old enough to count pennies."

"Better to be stupid than a thief," Cathy said softly.

"Nor bright enough to know the difference!" Gert said, and raised her fist.

Wilt took a long, slinking step toward Cathy. His smile shone brilliant in his coaled face. "Beatin' up never made anybody bright, Gert." He laid a surprisingly clean hand on Cathy's shoulder. "It's love and fondness makes ladies think the right way, and you know it, Gert."

Across the little room, Gwilym stood entirely still, his eyes fixed on Cathy.

Gert lowered her hand, and suddenly giggled. She flapped her apron and went back behind the counter. "What is it down in them mines that makes you gentlemen so jaunty when you come up?" She picked up one of the day-old loaves, held it out to Gwilym. He turned his head slowly, and then, without smiling, reached for the bread.

"Please, Wilt . . ." Cathy said.

Gwilym turned on them. Wilt had his arm locked around Cathy's shoulder; she was trying to squirm away, but couldn't. With a deliberate calm, Gwilym said, "Knock it off, Wilt."

Wilt said, in Cathy's ear but quite out loud, "I'll let you go if you give me a kiss—one little sisterly kiss."

Gwilym said, *"Och y fi,* man! Ain't this town dirty enough? Can't you leave a thing clean's you found it?"

"Distract my friend, Gert. He annoys me."

The Sixth Finger

Gert laughed aloud, an ugly, braying sound. Cathy tried again to pull free of Wilt, but he held her tight, and tried to get his grubby cheek near hers.

Gwilym took a step, laid both hands on Wilt's arm and wrenched it from Cathy. Wilt gave a grunt and aimed a punch at Gwilym, who blocked it easily and slammed his own fist into Wilt's middle. Wilt wheezed and dropped to his backside, dazed.

Cathy brushed at the handprints on her dress. She looked at Gwilym. "Thank you, Gwilym."

He met her eyes for a split second, and then turned back to Gert, who was still dumbly holding the bread. Gwilym took it, nodded, and put a shilling on the counter.

Gert snatched up the money and put it in the cash box. Then she pulled a length of paper from a roll and wrapped another loaf in it. She thrust it at Cathy. "Well! If the Englishman wants another loaf, take it to him!"

"And I bring you a bob for day-old, is that so, Gert? Not a bob two for fresh?"

Her jaw tight, Gert fetched a pencil from her apron and scrawled "1/-" on the parcel.

Cathy took it, stepped toward the door. "*Bore da*, Gwilym," she said, and nodded just slightly to him, not looking at Gert at all.

"Wait," Gwilym said. "I'm going that way. I'll walk you." Moving much more awkwardly than he had a minute before, he opened the door and held it for Cathy.

After the door closed behind them, Wilt got to his feet, a hand on his belly. Gert crossed her arms and glared at him.

With the same good humor as before, Wilt said, "I forgive him. No man can be his own friendly self what just got fired from the only job in the world." He picked up a loaf of bread, spun a coin on the counter, and munched as it glittered and rang.

Gwilym led the way up the slope to the Ives house. Cathy walked a few steps behind, the bread tucked under her arm.

At the beginning of the walkway to the house, Gwilym stopped. "This is it, ain't it."

"Yes, Gwilym."

"I'll wait for you." He looked around, nervously, then sat down on a rock, hands folded between his knees.

Cathy said, "You're not going back to work this morning?"

"Ah well," Gwilym said. He pulled a cloth from his pocket and wiped his face with it, more rearranging than removing the coal dust. "First the foreman tells the manager that I've been makin' trouble among the miners, 'spreadin' discontent'—so he says—and actin' meself superior. The manager asks me if I'm some kind'a Red, that being his idea of cleverness, an' I say no, just black as the next fella." He spat into the bushes.

"Now, for that manager any man who can make a better joke than him must be not only a Red union or-gan-i-zer but a bomb-throwin' anarchist, so up I'm sent the heavenly stairs to Mr. Caradoc himself, the fat—" He stopped, shook his head. "Accomp'nied, look you, by one of the Constable's men, just in case I've brought me anarchist bomb along in me trousers. So once we're all friendly, Caradoc asks if I think I'm too good for his job, and I think aloud as maybe I am. So it's down tools for me, and led off the property by the law with 'is pistol.... So there's no work for me to go back to this morning, or tomorrow morning, or the day after."

Cathy stared. In the town, the mine was work: the banker had his job, yes, and Jones, and Reverend Williams, but any other man—"Oh, Gwilym...."

Gwilym stood up, shouted down the valley, "And pleased to turn my back on Caradoc and his hole in the ground! I wish I could turn it on this whole town. Forever!" He turned back to Cathy. He was smiling crookedly, and seemed to be struggling with some idea he could not quite speak. "When you stand up here, y'see ... how much bigger the Rhondda is than that little black town. And if you could get even higher up, like ... in an airplane, the world would be bigger still. No end to bigness, and no end of better things for a man to do than dig with his hands, and sleep bad in a bed full of coal dust and gelignite, an die coughin' black an' bloody. But naught else you can see of it from down there, in the pit, in the hole...."

"Where would you go, then?"

"Anywhere, anywhere *forward*. Anywhere out from under—away from all this dirt and stupidity—and from the black mine that's to blame for it all! It is like a disease, see, spreadin' out under the ground, eatin' up everything, *killing*—" He turned away from her again. "Days I think the greatest thing would be to see it all blown to flinders."

"You'll go forward, Gwilym. You're smarter than the others—"

Still looking away, he said, "Smart enough to leave myself with no living." He turned slowly, enough to look sidewise at her. "But if there's one to be found, maybe smart enough to find it."

With a sudden shock, Cathy realized that Gwilym meant to leave—not just Caradoc's mine, but the town—perhaps the valley, for some impossibly larger world. "I wish I was smart as you—"

"Oh," Gwilym said gently, "You're . . . maybe not educated, see, but not stupid—you could learn, if there were anything to be learned here. That's the big difference between you and the others . . . that's why I—"

She waited.

Gwilym said, "I'll find somethin', see, where me brains count for somethin'. And I'll come back then. I'll come back in a big white car, y'see, bigger than Caradoc's, wearin' a fine suit and a gold ring, and I'll—"

Again Cathy waited. Behind them, wood creaked, and she turned. Professor Mathers was standing on the house's front porch, blinking in the daylight. There was no way to guess how long he had been standing there, what he had heard. He gave a small, embarrassed nod, went back inside and closed the door.

Gwilym said, "So that's the *Saesneg* Professor."

"Don't use that word, Gwilym."

"Och, no politics in it. I don't hate Englishmen." His face twisted up. "A man ought to know what he hates."

"Gwilym," Cathy said in a sudden rush of inspiration, "What if you asked him for a job?"

"If I *what*? What would I be with him, then? His butler maybe?"

"No, no! He told me just this mornin'— He needs an as-sis-tant. It's a smart man that's needed for such work. It'd be just the thing—and right here, and—"

Gwilym stared at the house. He ran his hand through his hair, as if combing it into place. "Here, Cathy . . . see what you can do t'make me presentable."

~~~~~~~~~~~

Mrs. Ives knocked sharply at the laboratory door and opened it without waiting for an answer. Inside, Mathers looked up from a microscope eyepiece.

Mrs. Ives said, "Excuse me, Professor. It's young Cathy here to see you. I told her—"

"Cathy? Show her in."

"Professor?"

"Yes, right away, thank you."

Mrs. Ives blinked, then went back into the hall. A moment later, Cathy entered. Mrs. Ives's shadow still fell across the doorway.

"Cathy," Mathers said kindly, "I'm afraid that I must disappoint you. It's—the way your cells are."

"Oh," she said, in a small voice. "I'm not—sick, am I?"

"Not at all. You know that different people have different blood types, don't you? This is like that."

"Ah. But you see, it wasn't for that I come—I did bring your bread, Mrs. Ives has it—but—" She stepped forward, and Mrs. Ives stepped aside, and Gwilym came into the room. "Here is my friend, Gwilym Griffiths—"

Gwilym said clearly, "Cathy here says you're in want of an assistant. I come to apply for the job."

Mathers put on his glasses, examined Gwilym. "Do you think you're qualified for this particular job?"

"I can do anything another bloke will do, and maybe better, come you! Just give me a chance, and I'll prove it."

"Very well. I'm working with high-frequency electronics on a molecular level. Are you familiar with solid-state circuitry? Have you read Prokop and Christopher on micro-acoustic masering? Or even Mathers on mitochondrial resonance?" He smiled. "But you're right, I spoke of an assistant, not a collaborator. Very well: any experience in ordinary lab technique? Microscopy, fixing and staining? Biopsy? Protein analysis and synthesis? Warewashing? Any background in office work—keypunch, filing procedures? Can you type? Oh, Mrs. Ives, that *will* be all, thank you."

Gwilym stood still, fists clenched, until Mrs. Ives had gone up the stairs. Then he said, hotly, "Are you tryin' to make a fool of me?"

Quietly and seriously, Mathers said, "No. On the contrary, I'm trying to suggest that you're best adapted to what you've been doing. That is much kinder than offering you work that you would soon discover was beyond your depth. Believe me, I know what that is like."

Gwilym turned round, his shoulders hunched. Cathy caught his arm, and he stopped, but did not look at her.

Cathy said, "If you teached that monkey to do some of your work . . . couldn't you teach Gwilym, who is smarter than anyone else in town?"

"Monkey—?" Gwilym said, bewildered.

"I'm sure Gwilym could learn to file papers, but Darwin can do that." Mathers sighed, and his shoulders sagged. "I was a pretty good teacher, when I was a teacher—just as I was a pretty good MD when I did that. But I'm doing something beyond that, here."

"If it's man's work—" Gwilym said.

"Well," said Mathers with a small smile, "I'm not sure it is." He looked at the wall, at a framed picture of a group of men standing outside a blank, fenced building. "We have developed our knowledge faster than we have evolved the intelligence to use it. We can build weapons of mass death, but only here and there is there an understanding of what mass death means for humanity. Perhaps in a thousand years—or ten thousand—we'll know better; but we don't have a thousand years. . . .

"But possibly—the same way we accelerated the engines of destruction—we can supercharge the engines of evolution. Beat the deadline."

He looked at Cathy and Gwilym. They had not moved; they were watching him, Gwilym with open-faced interest, Cathy with something like wonder. "As an embryo develops," he said intently, "undifferentiated cells follow instructions to form complex structures—organs and tissues. Even after a human being is born, it isn't quite finished—the skull fuses, growth continues. But at some point, the developmental instruction set runs out, and the cells simply repeat themselves. It takes another generation for anything new to happen, and a human generation is, by the standards of most life on Earth, terribly long. I'm trying to pry into the genetic mechanism—issue new instructions. We could move farther along an evolutionary line *within a single lifetime.*"

Mathers looked at Darwin the chimp, who sat placidly atop the filing cabinet. "I brought Darwin to a nearly human intelligence. If I could *begin* with a human intelligence, expand it in the same way—perhaps we could get control of the power we already have, use it for what we used to call the good of mankind."

Gwilym said, in a quiet voice, "An' I was always told evolution was about monkeys turnin' into men. . . ."

"Nothing like it," Mathers said. "My friend Darwin—even before I enhanced him—was as highly evolved as you or I, or a horse, or an oak tree. But, thousands of generations ago, our ancestors each took different roads. Ours got opposable thumbs and larger brains; his didn't. It was purely an accident of birth, followed by accidents of who was better at reproducing." Mathers looked at the monkey with something much more than a pet-owner's affection; with respect. "It's entirely possible that some of his ancient grandsires were born with big brains, started on the road to what we smugly call human intelligence, but their cousins—our forerunners—saw that as a threat, and wiped out the smart ones. Intelligence is a wild card in the survival game—and we must hope that it is a survival trait in our hand, because it seems to be the only one that *homo*-semi-*sapiens* has left."

Gwilym looked at Darwin, then at Mathers. Stiffly, hesitantly, he said, "What if you—began—with me?"

"You—?"

"Aye."

Mathers looked from Gwilym, to the glass-windowed chamber in the corner of the laboratory, then back again. "You're aware that this would be an experiment on the cells that make up your body? That if it failed, it could cripple you terribly—if it didn't simply kill you?"

"Every man down that pit's crippled sooner or later, and we all die in our time. I'm game for anything, sooner than go scrape before the fat man, askin' his leave t'crawl back down his bloody pit."

Mathers waited for a minute or more, looking at one of his blackboards. Then he called, "Mrs. Ives!" and in a clatter of shoes from just at the top of the stairs, the housekeeper was back in the doorway. "Yes, Professor?"

"Take the young man upstairs and clean him up. Fix him the bed in the library. He's going to be staying with us for awhile."

Mrs. Ives blinked.

Mathers said evenly, "I will of course be paying for his board. And I believe I am already renting the entire house."

Mrs. Ives smiled then, just a little. "This way, then."

As Gwilym passed Cathy, he paused, and stretched out a hand toward her cheek. An inch from touching it, he looked at his fingers, grimy and black-veined with coal dust. He rubbed them together, smiled at her, and went out.

~~~~~~~~~~~~~~~

Gwilym ran a comb through his just-washed hair. It was straight, and yellow—almost as golden as Cathy's, once the dust was out of it. He looked into the mirror: his face was even and still smooth, and he liked to suppose he was still a good-looking fellow, at least when he was clean.

It had been a long time since Gwilym had been this clean. The showers at the mine were just pipes, with a carbolic soap, so you could go home and not turn your sheets to mud. After a few years down the pit, it was a dye in your flesh, darkening you like an old tintype picture, dwelling in your lungs so your spittle came up black.

He dressed in the clothes Mrs. Ives had brought up: they were all white, like a doctor's clothes, shirt and trousers and a long jacket, white rubber-soled shoes. His pit clothes were lying in the corner. In the clean white cloth, Gwilym didn't want to get near them. They ought to be burned, he thought. There was half a scuttle of coal in them anyway.

Through the unwashed window, he could see the minehead, standing above the town like an iron tombstone. He couldn't entirely explain to himself why he hated it so—it was something more than the dirt, and the grinding work, and the smug airs of the fat, stupid men who had power over you there. After all, he had hardly known anything else in his life; his father had died in a premature blast when Gwilym was sixteen, and his mother hadn't lived much longer. Maybe, he thought, you had to be truly close to something, have it inside you, to hate it so.

But then, there was Cathy. Maybe there was more than hate inside him.

He went downstairs to the laboratory. Mathers had put on a clean white coat himself, and had a hypodermic tray laid out.

"Good," Mathers said. "Now, we have to see if you can meet the limitations of the hardware. Take off your coat and roll up your sleeve; I need to draw some blood from you."

Gwilym did so. Then he held a gauze over the needle mark while Mathers fiddled with his microscope.

Mathers looked up, his face thoughtful.

Gwilym said, "Do I pass, Professor?"

"You'll do."

Gwilym nodded. "Let's get it started, then."

"No reason to wait."

Gwilym looked around the room, at the metal booth in the corner. "How do you do it? Is it shots? Or—" He put his fingertips to his temple, suddenly a little less confident.

"No, there's no surgery." Mathers went to a bank of particularly massive machines. "These are hypersonic frequency generators. They stimulate cell division and protein synthesis, but selectively—" He paused, started over. "We're going to stimulate the growth of complex structures in your cells, mainly your brain and central nervous system, using some of the same codons—

assembly instructions—that caused you to develop from an embryo."

Mathers touched a large control handle, labeled with degree markings and the words FORWARD and REVERSE. "The control system is internally very complicated, but it all reduces to this. The division marks represent about five hundred generations—ten thousand years of natural evolution."

"It can go backward, too?"

"The cells retain some of the old codons. The same procedure can reactivate those. So yes, within some limits, we can go back." He turned to look Gwilym straight in the eye. "Though I warn you, it's not like turning pages back and forth in a book. More like welding a bridge together, and then taking it apart again." He took a breath. "This is an experiment. If it fails, you will very likely die before anything can be done to save you. It's no mark against you if you want to give it up."

Gwilym's hands tightened. Then he walked purposefully to the booth, swung the door open, and entered. He sat down on the chair within, and looked straight out through the glass.

Mathers nodded. He pressed sweating palms against his lab coat, then went to the master control. He pushed it two divisions forward.

Power built in the system. The dull whine of dynamos and hum of high-frequency electronics was joined by a high-pitched tone that seemed to resonate in the bone marrow. A dozen green traces, with cryptic annotations, drew themselves across oscilloscope screens.

Through the glass, Gwilym's form began to blur. He gripped the arms of the chair, and his mouth opened, clearly in pain. Mathers reached for the dial, but Gwilym's eyes opened and he shook his head vigorously, clamping his mouth shut, holding himself taut and still.

The oscillating green traces began to flatten out. When they had reached shallow sine waves, Mathers eased the master control back to center. He pulled switches, and the orange glow of the power tubes faded.

Mathers went to the chamber window. Gwilym was sitting hunched forward, his face buried in his hands. Most of his hair had fallen out, and his bare forehead had grown bulbous, at least two inches higher than before. On his hands, the knuckles had grown more prominent, the musculature more developed and complex, the fingers longer—and on each hand was the stubby beginning of a sixth finger.

Gwilym lowered his hands. His cheekbones had grown more prominent, and his eyes were greatly enlarged—great and luminous, like a newborn's eyes.

He stood, looking around as if disoriented. Mathers ran to open the chamber door.

Gwilym emerged, to stand half a span taller than Mathers. He reached to his shoulder, brushed away a clump of fallen hair. His cheek bulged as he ran his tongue around his mouth; then he held his palm to his mouth and spat out four gray molars and a bit of blood.

"Me wisdom teeth," Gwilym said thickly, and laughed. Then he looked down at Mathers, smiling from somewhere very far away. "Ye're so full of guilt, Professor," he said. "It drips off you like sweat. Am I s'posed to ease the guilt, then? Well. We'll see. Lots to see—an' I can see so much more now."

He took a step, nearly stumbled, but caught himself with an almost balletic grace. "But I've come a long way, and now we must look at where I've got to."

~~~~~~~~~~

Mrs. Ives came out of the kitchen with two meat pies and a pot of coffee on a tray. The day had gone, darkness had come, and the Professor and the town boy were still shut up in the laboratory.

She listened at the door, as she had done every half hour since the awful machine noise had finally stopped, but still heard nothing clearly.

She kicked the door. "It's Mrs. Ives, Professor. I've brought your dinner tray—for you and the young man."

Mathers's voice came through the closed door: "Leave it outside, Mrs. Ives. We can't be interrupted."

"As you like, sir. . . . Don't let it go cold!"

"Thank you, Mrs. Ives. Good night."

Mrs. Ives put the tray down, took a few deliberately noisy steps back, and then waited. But the door did not open, and finally she gave in and went to bed.

~~~~~~~~~~

Mathers went back to his notebook, made a few more entries, then put his pencil down, suddenly weary. "It would be . . . premature for her to see you, I think."

Across the room, Gwilym was sitting calm and still in his lab whites, looking at his reflection in a full-length mirror. A few feet away, Darwin the chimp was crouched, watching Gwilym with what seemed to be fascination.

Gwilym said, "You didn't tell me that my body would change."

"I hadn't expected such major changes in only twenty thousand years." Mathers paused, tapped his notebook. "In a way, it's very hopeful; it means we're closer to the end of an equilibrium period than I'd thought."

Gwilym looked at Darwin. "Why didn't he change?"

"When I enhanced Darwin, I had an earlier version of the equipment, not as precise or powerful. And, too, his species may be caught on an equilibrium level—an evolutionary plateau." He went to stand beside Gwilym, examining him before the mirror. "Your forebrain has almost doubled in size. And your eyes—do you notice real improvements in your vision?"

"Aye. I can see much farther to the sides. And everything looks brighter."

"The eyes are very closely coupled to the brain." Mathers took Gwilym's hand. "Your hands are clearly stronger and more dexterous. The sixth finger . . . polydactyly is well-known, but we tend to think of it as a birth defect. Perhaps it's a sort of progress that's never been able to take hold."

"It is a high price to pay for power over other men," Gwilym said plainly.

Mathers said, "Power?"

"Isn't that what it's about, Professor? Better men, smarter men, stronger men, who can do more than hope to make things better? Ach, now I've frightened you again. You're beginning to think you've made a monster."

Mathers let Gwilym's hand drop and took a step back. "Telepathy?" he said.

"Y'don't believe in mind-reading, do you, Professor?" Gwilym shut his huge eyes for a moment—it was like lights going out in the room—and then said, "I don't know, truly. It's not like words comin' to me over the radio. It may be I'm just seein' things others miss." He sniffed the air. "And smellin' em. You stank of fear there, though I didn't know till now that was what it was." He chuckled. "Twenty thousand years to learn what a dog's born knowin'." He looked at his hands, flexed the inch-long new fingers. "What should we find out next?"

~~~~~~~~~~~~~~

When Mrs. Ives came downstairs in the morning, the dinner tray was still outside the door, dead cold. She tapped her foot. If the Professor wanted to pay for food and not eat it, all very well, but *still*—

She knocked on the parlor door. "Professor Mathers?"

"What is it?"

"Are you all right? You ain't touched your dinner tray, an' it's stood 'ere all night!"

"We're too busy to stop. Take it away."

She took it back to the kitchen, trying to think what to do with the cold food. Mathers had always been quite willing to drink reheated coffee as if it were fresh, so there was some economy, but the mutton had congealed, its fat gone rancid, so that a cat wouldn't eat it. Never mind that unnatural monkey.

There was a knock at the front door. Mrs. Ives plunked the tray down and went to answer it. It was Cathy Evans, with the morning's new bread.

"*Bore da,* Mrs. Ives. I've brought you two loaves . . . one for Gwilym, you see."

"Very well. That'll be two shillings fourpence, then? I'll get my purse."

Cathy took the money with a small curtsy, but did not leave the porch. She said, "And how is Gwilym keepin' himself?"

"Now there's a question. They haven't either come out of my parlor since they started up yesterday. Haven't eaten, or—it's peculiar, that's what it is. Like the business with that monkey. Strange and peculiar. But I'll find out, I will . . . ."

Cathy said, "If you might tell him . . . Gwilym, I mean . . . that I'm come . . . ."

"You? What for? Do *you* know what they're doin' in there? I think a person ought t'know what goes on in her own house."

Cathy swallowed. "No—not really, Mrs. Ives. I'd just like to see Gwilym, if I may. If you'd tell him I'm here—"

"Well, I'll tell him, but you'll see what good it does." She took Cathy's hand and practically dragged her through the door, slamming it shut behind. She went to the laboratory door and banged on it.

Mathers handed Gwilym a clipboard with a dozen sheets of paper on it. Gwilym glanced at the document, raised a pencil, and began checking off response boxes one after the other, without an instant's hesitation. In less than a full minute, he had completed the work and handed it back.

Mathers opened the answer key to the intelligence test, compared the first few answers, then tossed it aside. "I wonder if this counts as publishable results," he said dryly.

"You seem disappointed," Gwilym said.

"No. And I'm not really surprised. Our tests already fail to mean much at the highest levels of human intelligence. For you, they're only proof that you're not testable. Which is certainly no cause for disappointment." He shook his head. "It just leaves me wondering where to go next."

"Knowledge is next, Professor. I have intelligence now, but what good can it do me without knowledge?"

"Yes, I see what you mean."

"I think maybe y'do. You said you had a library upstairs. I want those books. I want 'em like a starvin' man wants food."

"Shall we start with—"

"I don't *care* what we start with! Just bring me the books—I want 'em *all*."

Mrs. Ives's fist hit the door. "*Mis*-ter *Griff*-iths! Y'have a visitor!"

Something like pain flashed in Gwilym's eyes. Quietly, he said to Mathers, "That'll be Cathy. She can't see me."

Mathers said, "I'm sorry, Mrs. Ives, but we really can't be disturbed."

Out in the hallway, Cathy whispered, "Tell him it's me."

"It's Cathy that is come by," Mrs. Ives said.

Gwilym's voice came through the door. "Go away! I have—things I must be doing!"

Mrs. Ives folded her arms and looked at Cathy with deep satisfaction.

Cathy straightened her shoulders, plucked neatly at her shawl. "He's right, he is, not to have the likes of me breaking in on his studies. He's—*important* things to do."

And she left the house, clutching the bread money.

~~~~~~~~~~

In the Evans bakery, Wilt Morgan had come in for his morning meal of day-old bread, and now was playing a whiny jig on a tiny concertina. He had bought it more than a year ago at a fair, and knew three dancing tunes, all of which sounded pretty much alike, and "Men of Harlech," which sounded like nothing on Earth. As he played, Gert sat across the counter, looking into space, her fingers keeping idle time on the cash box.

Wilt said, "Sing, Gert. It's been years since I heard yer tender voice."

Gert smiled. It was a thing few people saw, and those few were usually startled by its prettiness. "What've I to sing about? Oh . . . ." The smile went away. "It's a funeral dirge I'd be singing—for all the lost things."

The doorbell jangled as Cathy came in. Gert said, "Speakin' of lost things! Where've you been?"

"Delivering the bread, Gert."

"All this time?" There was nothing left of the smile now. Gert turned to Wilt. "What do you do with a plain-faced liar?"

Wilt picked up the dance tune again. It might have been meant to be melancholy, or might have just come out that way. "Plain-faced? I wouldn't say plain-faced, Gert . . . I'd say touching . . . maybe even pretty." His mouth drooped into a mask of tragedy. "Yes. Pretty. In a sad way."

Cathy stood very still. Her lower lip trembled, almost too slightly to see.

"Go on!" Gert said. "There's enough to do for three of you! Get a move on!"

Wilt said, "Speak to her gently, Gert. She's hurtin' enough, these days."

Cathy started toward the back of the shop, but Wilt grasped her arm. "You are, aren't you?"

"Please, Wilt—"

"Gwilym gone off to seek his fortune, and no doubt without even a kiss for his fair lady . . . that must be hurtin' you real deep."

Gert broke into her awful, unsmiling, donkey laugh. "Ah, leave her go, Wilt. She ain't never been fair lady to no one. An' Gwilym never but looked clean through her, though she didn't know any better."

"Stop it," Cathy said, trying to control her voice. "Please. Stop it."

Wilt's eyes widened. He let her go.

She took a step back, then stood her ground. "Gwilym's *not* forgot me, do you hear? But he's very busy . . . he's *got* work, and important work, and he's tryin' to . . . better himself. Yes, tryin' to make himself something more than any of us could ever be!"

Wilt looked almost thoughtful for a moment, then burst out laughing like a steam whistle. "Well, now! Ain't that typical! The little thing finally speaks her piece, and who does she speak it for? A rotter what can't even hold down a job in an honorable profession! So what's the man going to be, then? Another Nye Bevan? Come to lead us all to the Promised Land?"

"Aye," Gert said, laughing too, "an' he'll hold up the sky with his broad shoulders. . . ."

"Stop it!" Cathy shouted, and the laughter did stop. "You may laugh at me, but you may not laugh at Gwilym. He is not to be laughed at!"

Then Wilt's laughter started again, merry and all the meaner for it. He began pumping on the concertina: "Alllll—throoo—the niiiiight—" Cathy stared at him, the tears starting to break free of her eyes; then she struck at him, slapping the little squeezebox from his hands. It hit the floor and collapsed, breathing out a dying chord.

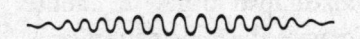

Mathers heard music.

He lifted his head from the laboratory desk. It was nearly dark; he must have fallen asleep hours ago. His glasses were askew on his face; he adjusted them and looked around, but Gwilym was not in the room.

And the sound of Bach was floating down the stairs.

Mathers went upstairs. The music was coming, not from the record player in the library, but from the little piano room that Mrs. Ives insisted was a "conservatory."

Inside, Gwilym was playing a Bach fugue with masterly precision, his eyes fixed on the complicated sheet music, his long, thin hands floating spiderlike over the keys.

"Come in, Professor," he said, without missing a note.

Mathers went slowly forward.

Still playing, Gwilym said, "I am looking back across time, Professor. It is as wonderful as . . . Carter opening Tutankhamen's tomb, or the first Western view of Angkor Wat. . . . I do wish that you had more books on archeology." There was no longer any trace of Welsh in his voice; it was precise, uninflected, almost mechanical.

"I'll . . . see what I can do."

"It is fascinating to see what retains its power over millennia—many millennia. This simple fugue, for instance. . . . Bach shall quite probably outlive us all." He stopped, flipped pages to another piece, and began again, with the same perfection.

"I had no idea you could play this well," Mathers said, although he already knew the answer.

"I have never before touched the keys of a piano, Professor. But playing the piano is only a matter of mathematics—was not Bach the great mathematician of sound?—and, to a certain degree, manual dexterity. Also, this piano is badly out of tune, and I am being forced to compensate." He stopped again, changed music and began. "Man produces very little that is lasting. Truly lasting. It is understandable."

"You understand it?" Mathers said, feeling tiredness sweep over him again.

"You are afraid of being different. You are afraid of being wrong in ways that will bring punishment. Worse, you are afraid of being thought wrong. All this drains creative energy. And when we give up our creative energy, we do not create. We procreate," he added, with a sudden, unreadable inflection, "but we do not create."

"Procreation is the engine of evolution," Mathers said, the line floating up from a lecture long, long ago, when he had been a fair excuse for a teacher.

"An engine. Indeed."

"I must . . . I must get some sleep."

"Yes. You must."

"Your playing won't disturb me."

"I shall stop soon, anyway."

"Goodnight, then."

"Goodnight, Professor."

Mathers stumbled down the stairs to his bedroom, took off his lab coat and his shoes, and fell over on his unkempt bed. He stared at the ceiling. He drifted into troubled sleep.

He awoke to moonlight and the sound of his door opening.

"Who's there?"

Gwilym was standing in the doorway, holding two enormous stacks of books. Each pile was balanced perfectly on one open palm; he carried them as if they weighed nothing. "I've finished these books."

Mathers squeezed his eyes shut against the moon. "It's the middle of the night, Gwilym. Why aren't you asleep?"

"I no longer have any need to sleep."

A little more awake now, Mathers turned his head. Gwilym was reshelving the books.

Suddenly Mathers was fully conscious. He got out of bed and went to Gwilym, taking hold of Gwilym's right hand. The fingers had lengthened by at least half an inch, and the muscles developed even further.

And the sixth finger was as long as the others.

"But this—when did this happen?"

"Within the last three or four hours, I believe. I was too absorbed in reading to notice."

"But you're—continuing to develop. Outside the chamber."

"You are tired, Professor. You are not thinking clearly. You said yourself that I had left an equilibrium level. You gave my developmental mechanisms instructions to proceed; you did not tell them to stop."

Mathers tried to organize his thoughts. He held Gwilym's fingers delicately, feeling curious currents of warmth. "How does it . . . feel?"

"If I concentrate, I can perceive the microstructures building and changing—in a gross and imperfect way, but enough to understand the overall process. It is . . . somewhat painful . . . *ah*." He smiled, and to Mathers's sleep-clouded eyes the light level in the room seemed to increase. "My sensorium is beginning to compensate. Within an hour I will no longer sense it as pain."

Mathers pinched the bridge of his nose. The soft light around Gwilym remained.

"Yes, Professor. I have brought my own light. I had not noticed it until now. It is the small waste energies of molecular bonds breaking and reforming. If my ATP cycle were not vastly more efficient than the human, I should have the appetite of twenty men."

Gently, Gwilym took his hand away from Mathers, looked at it, gestured toward Mathers's books with it. "I have read your books now—the ones you considered important enough to bring to Wales—and I understand more of your mind, which makes it much more clearly readable. You have Teilhard de Chardin right next to Darwin and Wallace. Whatever orthodoxy may claim, or you may profess, Professor, you believe that evolution is not really blind. You believe that we are on an ascent, and that is how you structured your machine: to affirm your heresy." He laughed then; it sounded like cathedral bells, echoing and distant.

"Are you laughing at me?" Mathers said, and the laughter stopped. Mathers wondered if he would ever hear it again.

"At this immense guilt of yours, Professor—or should I say Doctor? You were always Dr. Mathers until a few years ago. I understand guilt, Doctor—I assure you, I have forgotten nothing—but I do not understand the sources of *your* guilt." He looked at the door to the laboratory. "There is a group photograph in there, yourself and other scientists. There are mysterious citations in your books—will you tell me what the Gamma-Delta Project is?"

Mathers groaned.

Gwilym said, "Yes?"

Mathers sat down on the edge of the bed. "It was a weapon. The Genetic-Shift Device. Do you know what a neutron bomb is?"

"An atomic weapon intended to make a great deal of radiation, increasing the number of human casualties."

"Yes. The Gamma-Delta was to be even more specific. It would generate radiation that would have maximum effect on human genetic material—like those the chamber in the laboratory uses, but uncontrolled, *deliberately* uncontrolled."

"Teratogenic radiation," Gwilym said.

"That's right. Monsters. And not in the next generation, as the ordinary weapons would already do, but *right now*. In a *hurry*. Everyone in its wake transformed to viscid, spiny, flapping things, afraid to go near one another lest their touch breed something even worse. It would have done more than kill people: it would have erased humanity from all it did not kill."

"'Science is not everything,'" Gwilym said, "'but science is very beautiful.'"

"Don't quote Oppenheimer at me!" Mathers said, suddenly angry. "I *knew* him—" Then he shook his head. "We saw what we were doing. The only way we drove ourselves to work on the thing was the thought—"

"That it would be, finally, too terrible for humans to use on other humans?" Gwilym said with heartless calm.

"No. No, there are limits to self-deception. The thought that some good use could be made of the work. A cure for the common cold."

"That is a quote from Enrico Fermi."

"It is. I knew him, too. So many good people gone."

Gwilym looked out the window, at the moon. "And was this device completed? Deployed?"

"No. We couldn't get the effect on a large enough scale to compete with ordinary enhanced-radiation weapons—which do the same thing, but not so well. And I think it finally dawned on someone that any enemy hit with the Gee-Delta would have literally nothing left to lose in retaliation. This is the way the world ends . . . ."

"Not with a bang, but a whimper," Gwilym said. "You had opened the book so many times to that poem, I knew it must mean something to you." He paused. "But you see . . . I am the only new life that you have created. And now you wonder if I am in fact the monster of your nightmares."

Mathers stood up. "We have to get you into the chamber again. Reverse the process, before we lose your old pattern entirely."

"My 'old pattern' is as far behind me now, Dr. Mathers, as the little proto-hominids who scuttled around the dinosaurs' feet are removed from you. Tell me plainly: would *you* enter the chamber and allow me to return you to *that?*"

Mathers sank back onto the bed. "What do you want, then?"

"More knowledge. More books. That is all I want now. In time, when I have enough knowledge, I will know what I want to do with it." He started to go, then paused in the doorway. "Am I hideous to you, Doctor?"

"No," Mathers said, in an exhausted voice. "To me you are beautiful, because when I look at you I still see hope."

~~~~~~~~~~~~~~

Mrs. Ives was tired of carrying books up the stairs. For days now, the post had been bringing crates of books for the Professor, but it wasn't him who carried them up to Gwilym's room. And he never stuck his nose out the door. Useless as he might be, the Griffiths boy had muscles enough to haul his own books. Anyway, half of them weren't even in English! What sort of fool did they take her for?

She dropped the stack by the door. "More books for ye, young man."

"Very well," he said—if it still was his voice, it sounded so high-and-mighty now. "Leave them."

Was this her house or wasn't it? She took heavy steps away from the door, then walked lightly back and stood against the wall, facing it, almost holding her breath.

The door swung slowly open. A hand like a huge, six-legged spider crept out, toward the books.

Mrs. Ives screamed.

Gwilym looked up. His head was a great, hairless sphere, twice the width of a normal man's, his eyes like blue lanterns in great frames of angular bone. His mouth was a small V, his chin pointed like a pantomime Devil's.

Mrs. Ives pressed herself hard against the wall, unable to draw enough breath to scream again. Finally she let out a strangled cry and lunged toward the stairs.

Gwilym wrapped his hand around her arm. "*Aros*," he said, his Welsh voice returned, his tone soft. "I won't hurt ye—"

She tried to pull free. Then, slowly, she turned to look him in the huge, glowing eyes.

She gasped, clutched her chest. She went rigid, and then limp; Gwilym lowered her to the floor and folded her arms.

In the hall below, the laboratory door opened, and Mathers appeared. He dashed up the stairs, looking in bewilderment from Mrs. Ives to Gwilym.

"Yes, Doctor. She is dead."

"How—?" Mathers said hollowly.

"She was too frightened even to run," Gwilym said. "The only thing that overcame that was her wish to share the fear with others, to bring a crowd here and overwhelm the horrible thing, destroy it." He looked down at Mathers. "I did not threaten her in any way. But does the little spider that you find unexpectedly in the bath offer you any threat, beyond its ugliness, its alienness?"

"So you killed her."

"My output of neural energy is sufficient to . . . cross the barriers to another's nervous system. I stopped the electrical activity of her heart . . . . It was not very painful. Only for an instant. It was not a thing that gave me any pleasure, Doctor."

"Or remorse, I suppose."

"I caused sufficient damage that her heart cannot be restarted. I did that to spare her pain. No possible emotion can alter physical events."

"No, but she was a human being—the same as ourselves."

Gwilym picked up the books. "The same as you, Dr. Mathers. A million years different from me."

~~~~~~~~~~

Only the vicar and a few of the townswomen sat in the church with Mrs. Ives's body. It lay on a bare board, in a bare hall, without a flower or a bit of crepe; just some naked candles for light and hope of the paradise to come.

Gert the Bread was sitting in the second pew, tugging at her best black shawl, rocking and declaiming: "Heart at-tack! Ha! She was strong as an ox! If that woman's heart stopped, it's because somebody put the fear of the Devil in her. And Gwilym Griffiths is just the one to . . . ."

Reverend Williams looked up from his book, his look angry and hopeless.

It certainly had no effect on Gert. "Wasn't she sayin' that there was something very peculiar going on up there? And she was going to get to the bottom of it? And look at her now, for only tryin' to find the honest truth in her own house! And th' town acts as if they believe that bloody Englishman, even if he does say now he's a proper doctor!"

There was a murmur of assent behind Gert. The vicar slammed his Bible shut and glared.

Gert said, "*I'll* speak no ill of the dead, thank you, Reverend. And after all it's nothin' to you; it's Constable Wilks I should be talkin' to."

Gert stood up, bowed slightly to the dead woman, and walked out. The others followed, until the only live people left in the church were the vicar and Cathy, who sat in the back pew, softly weeping.

Reverend Williams came down the aisle to stand by Cathy. "Of all here . . ." he said, "only one came to mourn. It is a good thing you have done, girl. Go on home, now."

She stood up, went out into the gray light. Had she come to mourn Mrs. Ives? she thought. Or another loss—

~~~~~~~~~~~~

Cathy ran all the way to the Ives house, and then up the stairs to Gwilym's room. There she paused, breathing hard, afraid to knock.

"Come in, Cathy," she heard Gwilym say.

She opened the door. Gwilym, in his gleaming white clothes, sat before the window, looking out; his head was obscured by a dazzling fog of white light.

"I am sorry now that I have been hiding," he said. "I can see now that it had no real purpose."

"I come to warn you . . . ."

"I know," he said. "The Constable has been called. Being Wilks, he will have sent two deputies, armed, in case it is labor trouble, or something political . . . I have forgotten nothing about this town." He shifted, his head still just a dark shape in radiance. "But you aren't afraid."

"What?" she said.

"Why aren't you afraid of me?"

"Oh, Gwilym—aren't we friends? You've always been kind to me . . . ."

Gwilym stood, and turned. The light was not coming from the window; it came from *him,* from skin like candlewax, from eyes like some great owl's, in a face that was a swollen demon-mask of angles and bones.

Cathy clasped both hands across her mouth, holding in her scream.

"I suppose I had some hope," he said, very softly. "But hope is unreason."

She turned and fled, practically tumbling down the stairs, seeing nothing, until suddenly she was gripped by hands, and she screamed uncontrollably.

"What's wrong?" a man shouted. Cathy got her eyes open. It was Mathers, holding her.

"I saw him—" She began to cry. Mathers led her into the laboratory, put her in a chair.

"What has happened to him?" she gasped. "What terrible thing have you done?"

"Cathy, you wouldn't understand . . . The experiment has gone too far."

"And is there nothing to be done? Is he—to be—like *that*? Never—my Gwilym—"

Hesitantly, Mathers put a hand on her shoulder. "I don't know, Cathy. Possibly—but—he would have to want to—"

She stared at him. "He doesn't *want* to—?"

A cry came from the hall outside, a scream, shrill and thin. Mathers pulled open a desk drawer, took out a revolver and slipped it into the pocket of his coat. He went out, Cathy a step behind him.

Darwin was crouching in the hall, looking toward Gwilym at its far end. When Mathers appeared, the monkey screeched again, pointed at Gwilym, and fled up the stairs. Cathy took an instant's glance at Gwilym, then turned away, into the laboratory. Mathers stood still.

Gwilym said, "I was having a conversation with Darwin."

"A *conversation*—"

"Come now, Doctor. You converse with him, however unsubtly. I was asking him about his attitude toward predators. I thought it would be useful to have another perspective, before proceeding."

"Proceeding with what?"

"The obliteration of the mine. And with it, the town. They have already sent their men, who will surely try to destroy me the moment they catch sight of me. I am going to do what your ancestors did when Darwin's ancestors showed signs of threatening them."

"And after them, what?" Mathers said, his voice breaking. "The next town, and the next? The war of extermination? The war to end war?"

"I have no doubt that if I offer that, it will be given me," Gwilym said calmly. "But my intention is only to give myself a little time. That is the weakness of your imperfect reason, Dr. Mathers. It requires time, reflection. When the human race pauses to think and consider—as when you walked away from the Gamma-Delta project to this little nowhere—it can achieve greatness. I do not hate humanity, Doctor. I admire its greatness. But it has all but abandoned its lust to greatness—Bach's, Leonardo's, Shakespeare's—in favor of all the other, lesser lusts. So you were right when you said that its time is short."

Mathers held still a heartbeat longer, and then drew his revolver. "Please," he said, "While you are still beautiful."

Gwilym inclined his head. The nimbus around him stretched out to enwrap Mathers, who was lifted off his feet and thrown like a rag doll into the corner of the hall, the gun flung away.

Gwilym walked down the hall and into the daylight, without a second glance at Mathers.

Cathy ran to Mathers's side. "Are you bad hurt, sir?"

Mathers shook his head, moved his limbs slowly and painfully. His muscles all felt strained. Gwilym's motor-nerve control had overpowered his own: Mathers had been made to throw *himself* across the hall.

Cathy said, "You called him beautiful."

It took Mathers some time to get control of his tongue. In a hoarse whisper, he said, "I suppose I did."

"You've changed him so—he used to walk with his feet firm on the ground, proud. Now he steps like he didn't want to touch earth at all. And his voice is a stranger's." She shook her head. "Then, I'm a stupid girl," she said slowly, "but I see the beauty too."

Mathers looked at her, caught up in wonder. Then he said, "I beg your forgiveness, Cathy. I underestimated you. When things come easy to a man, he'll do that—a strong man may hold a weaker one in contempt, one who grasps ideas easily may dismiss a slower one as stupid. I do it too often."

Cathy said, "There's never been man nor woman ever asked my forgiveness of anything, sir, but if you want it, it's yours."

"Thank you, Cathy. And you are not stupid. Never say so."

"Gwilym said that to me, when he was Gwilym." She looked at the open door. "He's grown strong now, hasn't he? He has a power in him."

"Yes."

"Well then," she said, her voice suddenly hollow and old, "if there's a thing on Earth he hates, sir, it's this town, and Mr. Caradoc's mine most of all. If he says he's gone to destroy them—then, sir, he has."

~~~~~~~~~~~~~

Caradoc, the president and chief stockholder of the Caradoc Mining Corporation (formerly Caradoc & Ives), liked to call himself "a man of settled appearance." Others, when he was not present, more often said fat, bald, and jowly.

His working office was built three floors above ground, with an enclosed back staircase for Caradoc and an open one out front for everyone else. It had big windows, so Caradoc could see the whole pithead complex, his imperial seat of steel girders and corrugated iron. He had to pay three women to keep the windows clean enough to watch through, as well as to get the dust out of the room—but it was honest work, more honest than simply sitting idle on a widow's pension.

Caradoc put down the telephone and sat back from his desk. It had been Wilks the Constable calling, something about trouble at the Ives house. Or at least that old hen Gert the Bread saying there was trouble. Caradoc supposed there was nothing to it. He hoped not. He was as Welsh as the next man—as much as King Harry the Fifth—but the Englishman, the Professor or whatever he was, had brought good money into the town, and taken Mrs. Ives off his mind.

Oh, aye, he thought, Mrs. Ives was dead. Just a day back. Heart. Well! Then the house would pass to the Corporation's ownership, and the Englishman's rents with it.

Caradoc thought he heard a footstep on the front stairs. He glanced at the side window, to see who it was, but the sun seemed to have caught a reflection and there was nothing visible but white light. Well. Probably just one of the foremen, reporting another of the same old grievances.

At least he was rid of the Griffiths boy. Not, truth be told, a bad worker. But he had bad ideas. Political ideas. Be unionizing in a year. You couldn't have that, a lazy man was better. A lazy man you could whip harder. But one with ideas—

The door opened. A figure all in white stood there, haloed in burning light, a vision. It had a bulbous head and eyes big as millwheels, pointed ears and a spike of a chin. As the breeze circled it, the dust itself seemed to be igniting around it. It walked in, its feet silent, in the sound of lightning and the smell of coal-fire.

"What . . . are you?"

"There is no name for what I am, not in this age," the thing said. Somewhere in Caradoc's mind, the voice seemed familiar. "All that still connects us is my loathing for this place, and for you, and all you do, and all you are."

Caradoc felt more confused than frightened. Men had walked into this office before, thinking a face-to-face demand would get them something. They soon learned better. But *this*—It just stood there. Didn't ask for anything. Caradoc could feel the hate from it, though, like the heat from a furnace.

Finally he said something he had hardly ever had to say, and he had to put all his strength into his voice to keep it even level: "What is it you want?"

The Devilish thing looked out the window, at the pithead and hoist. "You never would ventilate properly," it said. "That would cost money, and there was always a new set of lads to breathe the bad air after the old ones choked. Did you ever wonder what would happen if all the dust in Number Two were to take fire at once?"

"Couldn't happen," Caradoc said. He had said it so many times, to himself and others, that it came without thought. Then the thing turned back to him. And *smiled*.

"No," Caradoc said, suddenly shaking-afraid with the terrible possibility of it. "The whole pithead could collapse. And if Number Two vein caught—"

"The tunnels run beneath the town," the thing said. "Once the coal started to burn, no human power could put it out. The town above would be a little Hell for fifty years or more. Not that it has been anything less, for as long."

Caradoc kept a sawed-off shotgun in a bottom desk drawer. He had never had to use it. Now—if he could will himself enough to move—"Why would you do that?" he said, to try and distract the thing. "All those men down there—why would you do that?" Thinking of the gun made him think of Wilks's deputies. They were at the Ives house, but they would be coming back this way. Yes! They were coming. He had men coming. And if he wounded the thing, kept it here for them to take—there would be no question what kind of man Caradoc the Owner was then.

He got his fingers round the drawer pull—

"No," the thing said. "Not that drawer. *That* one."

Caradoc felt his arms suddenly seized by cramp. His hands rose up of themselves, and pulled open the upper left-side desk drawer. Then his right hand hovered, spread wide, before his face.

"That is the hand that holds the pen," the thing said, "that signed the cheques and the deeds, the dismissals and the foreclosures. The one that you think is life and death over men."

As if he were watching them from a great distance, Caradoc saw his right fingers wrap around the edge of the open drawer. Then his left arm recoiled and pistoned, slamming the drawer shut. Caradoc howled. He watched himself pull the drawer out and slam it again. Tears blinded him to the next blow, and the next, and the next.

The glowing thing opened the office door. As it departed, it said, "About one thing you were correct. Power cares nothing for the little men in its path."

Slowly, Caradoc lifted his wrecked hand from the drawer. He caught a glimpse of blood and raw bone, and could not bear to look at it again. He was nearly blind and deaf with pain.

He staggered against the desk, spilling papers, sending a water pitcher shattering to the floor. He got somehow to the open door, leaned against it. The smudge of glow was heading for the hoist, for Shaft Two.

The cord for the disaster whistle hung just outside the door. Caradoc got his left hand around it, and collapsed to the landing, pulling the cord down.

~~~~~~~~~~~~~~~

In the town, time stopped still. The click of typewriters in the bank, the scrape of chalk in the schoolhouse, the creak of metal as Jones the Fixit worked at an ancient toaster, all ceased in the same instant, cut dead by the sound of the whistle.

Because everyone knew what the whistle meant. There was trouble at the mine: fire, collapse, explosion. Men—and not just any men, but the men who lived in your house, who were the other parts of your life—crippled or dead or buried living under earth, waiting in absolute darkness for their air to go foul. The whistle was, simply, the sound of the worst thing in the world.

~~~~~~~~~~~~~~~

Wilt Morgan heard the whistle and came scrambling out of the shower room, struggling into his jacket and pants, without his boots. He looked up at the owner's office; there was a mound on the landing in the shape of Caradoc, its arm dangling over the edge.

And at the foot of the stairs was an apparition, burning with red and white fire.

It looked at him, *o Duw prid,* it *looked* at him, and began to walk toward him.

Wilt dropped to his knees, forcing his palms together, trying to remember the words he was supposed to know.

"No," it said. "You have no time for that. Run away, and tell other men what happened here."

Stumbling barefoot over the cinders and gravel, Wilt ran. As he neared the front gate, he met two men on motorcycles: the Constable's deputies. One of them pulled to a halt and shouted for Wilt to stop.

Wilt began to laugh hysterically, and kept running.

"What the devil was that?" the deputy said.

"The fear of death," the other one said.

"Ha'nt we ought see about the Ives place first?"

"Don't you hear the whistle, man? 'Gainst that, an old woman's tale counts for nothing."

Fifty yards further on they saw the white thing, walking with long, gliding strides toward the powder blockhouse.

"And what's—"

"Haven't you anything today but fool questions?" the other man said. "Come on."

They stopped their motorbikes, drew their revolvers, and advanced on the glowing man.

He turned to face them. The first deputy clamped both hands on his gun, leveled it, trembling.

Then he ceased to tremble, and did not fire. The second man turned to look at him, and then he too ceased moving.

The glowing man said, "Your ignorance makes me ill and angry. There will be an end to your savagery."

The two deputies faced each other. Their gun hands rose, slowly, until each man had his revolver's muzzle pressed directly against the other's forehead. Together they thumbed the hammers back. There they stopped. Only their eyes showed any animation: they were wide with terror.

Then the glowing man's aura shimmered and brightened. He put a six-fingered hand to his bulging forehead for a moment. He turned and began to walk away from the men, the powder house, the mine complex. He took a last glance at the office overhead, and the sound of the disaster whistle died away.

A few minutes later, the two deputies lowered their guns. They sagged, their muscles aching. They were too dazed to speak, even if there had been something to say.

A car came screeching through the mine gate. The first deputy started to raise his pistol again, but the other man shook his head, and they both holstered their weapons.

The driver was the Englishman from up the slope, Mathers. He emerged from the car, looked around. "What happened here?" he demanded. "Where is he?" There could be no doubt at all of who he meant.

The first deputy sat down hard on the ground and buried his face in his hands. The second said, "He was by the blastin' house, and then he turned on us . . . held us right in the palm of his hand. But then—it was as if he—changed his mind."

Suddenly Mathers leaned against the car and burst into shaking sobs. The deputy put a hand on his shoulder. "Man, are you—"

"I'm all right," Mathers said, straightening up, smiling as he wiped the tears from his face. "Changed his mind, yes," he said, to no one there. "There is still hope for us." He turned to face the deputy. "Will you come with me?"

"I don't know, sir—there's a man hurt up there, Mr. Caradoc himself from the looks of it."

"Oh," Mathers said. "Take me to him and I'll see what I can do—I'm a doctor, you see."

~~~~~~~~~~~~

Cathy sat in the middle of the laboratory, her arm around Darwin's brown-furred shoulder. After Mathers had gone, the chimp had come out of the kitchen with milk and biscuits on a tray, offering them to her. It had charmed her, overcome her fear. Now they were both waiting for—heaven knew what.

Darwin twitched, squeaked. Cathy looked up.

Gwilym stood in the doorway. He was another handsbreadth taller, his ankles showing below his white trousers. His skin was translucent: she could see webworks of vein and nerve like the leading in a stained-glass window. Sparks ran along the nerve trees, blood pulsed through vessels.

"Gwilym?"

"Cathy. . . . Please don't be afraid."

She tried not to be afraid. She held herself very still. "I heard the whistle. . . . Oh, my Gwilym, what have you done?"

"You are right. I meant to destroy the mine, the town, all and everyone within reach. And then, suddenly . . . I saw that it was only more waste, useless waste. It no longer mattered. I had no more use for hatred, or revenge, or even power." He gestured at Darwin, who nodded. "Do you see? Even Darwin is no longer afraid of me. And you are afraid, but without hate. Being without hate—I am so new to it, it seems a wonder as great as the physics that powers the stars." He smiled at her, said very gently, "I came back because you were here."

"Then that means . . . ." She could not say it.

"I have forgotten nothing. I did love you—"

Cathy started from her seat. Darwin whimpered and left the laboratory, closing the door behind him. Gwilym held up his hand. "—but now, I am like a man who remembers that his ancestors lived in a beautiful, vanished country . . . were kings in Atlantis. It could be that different things . . . wiser things . . . could have been done. But now it is lost, in the bittersweet past."

"*Then what?*" Cathy cried. "Why did you come back, just to hurt me so? You never—you never hurt me—"

"Because I need you," he said. "I am nearing an equilibrium level—the last plateau of life as matter. Once I break through that level, I shall no longer need a physical body. There will only be spirit . . . an intelligence freed of all material constraints." He looked upward. "Teilhard de Chardin dreamed of this, as men before him dreamed of angels . . . ."

"Angels?" Cathy said, terrified again.

"But I cannot wait to pass equilibrium. The call of infinity is too strong. And so I need your help." He pointed at the chamber. "I need a last enhancement. Another push through time. And you are the only one I can trust to help me.

"What can I say, Cathy? Mathers wanted to change the world, but the human world does not want to change, and if I—even if there were more like me—tried to force you to change, you would hate us to destruction." Gwilym pointed to the picture on the laboratory wall, of the men before the fenced building. "I think humanity would rather burn the world to radioactive ash than admit that they are not the endpoint of the entire universe. Well. If they outlive their terror, in a hundred thousand centuries they will find me waiting." He turned back to her, and his mouth opened in startlement. "You're . . . crying."

"I'm losing you! I'm losing you as I watch! You're turning into—this awful—" She reached toward him, her fingers just at the edge of his luminous aura, arching her feet to get closer to his eye level. "Come back to me, Gwilym—if you ever loved me, come back to me, the way you were. Don't you see? Whatever happens, however smart or powerful it makes you—*you'll be alone.*"

Gwilym paused. His face shifted form as Cathy watched. He seemed pleased, at a wonderful new thought.

"Yes . . . . It is something like tragedy, Cathy—a minute difference in your mitochondria, or you would have seen what I am seeing now, its unspeakable beauty. We could have gone forward together—the difference—" He held up his hands. "Of course, I wonder it took me so long to consider it." Then he shook his great head, slowly, with infinite sadness. "But there is not enough time. I could not gather the materials to build the tools to build the machines in time. Even if it could be done, then what? They would kill you, too, perhaps more easily, as the one who could breed—and if I saw that, I might learn hate again. . . . No. One experiment at a time."

He went to the master control bank, flipped the power switches. The amplifiers glowed to life. He touched the handle. "I could make you do it, Cathy . . . but I cannot. You have to want to help. Because . . . because I did love you. Truly."

She nodded, wiped her tears, went to the control.

Gwilym entered the chamber, bending to fit through the door. He tried to sit in the chair, then crouched beside it. "Forward now, Cathy. Forward all the way. . . . Goodbye, Cathy."

She put her hand on the control, moved it a hairsbreadth forward. The chamber generators began their keening, bone-deep whine.

"Please come back," she said. "Just enough to—to change things. Just come back enough to touch me, and I'll go with you, wherever it is. I'm not afraid. Not if I'm not alone."

She pushed the master control into REVERSE.

From within the chamber, Gwilym's enormous eyes widened still farther. His flesh began to shift like wax in the sun. His skull shrank. He spread his hands against the glass; the sixth fingers shortened, contracted. Cathy turned away, in terror. The generators shrieked like maddened violins.

"*Cathy!*" Gwilym screamed. "*Och, Cathy, os gwelwch yn dda—*"

She forced herself to look back. The hands on the glass were a man's hands again, and the face, though hairless and pale, was Gwilym's own.

Then it began to shift again, the nose flattening, the brow descending—

She cried out in horror and shoved the control to its center point, slapped at the power switches. The machines stuttered and groaned and kept on roaring, but the skull-shaking keening stopped.

She ran to the chamber door, pulled it open. Gwilym tumbled out, thudded to the floor and lay still. Cathy knelt, gathered him to her. His eyes were shut; he did not move. She could feel no breath or heartbeat.

"Gwilym," she said, just above a whisper. A tear fell from her eye to his cheek.

His eyes opened. He blinked against the harsh laboratory light. Slowly, awkwardly, he raised his hand to her face.

Professor Mathers came into the laboratory. His look was frightened and weary. Behind him, one of the Constable's men stood, bewildered, in the doorway.

Cathy looked up. "I brought him back. I think . . . he's glad. He touched me."

Mathers nodded. He went to the master board, touched the switches one by one, and the machine fell silent.

~~~~~~~~~~~

SINCE THE LATE 1970S, JOHN M. FORD *has been writing and publishing some of the most literate, original, and unforgettable science fiction, fantasy, horror, and suspense fiction the genres have ever known. His first novel,* Web of Angels, *is a clear source for much of the currently popular "cyberpunk" movement. as exemplified by William Gibson and Neal Stephenson. His first Star Trek® novel,* The Final Reflection *is unique in the Star Trek canon and quite possibly the best novel anyone has ever written to fit into a pre-existing universe.*

Ford has won two World Fantasy Awards, one for his novel The Dragon Waiting *and one for his long poem,* Winter Solstice: Camelot Station, *originally one of his legendary Christmas cards and now collected in* The Year's Finest Fantasy and Horror.

He lives in Minneapolis, Minnesota, where he is currently at work on a long novel entitled Aspects.